Benedict Kiely was born in 1919 in County Tyrone and settled in Dublin in 1944. After publishing his first book, *Counties of Contention* (a study of the partition of Ireland), he became a leader writer and columnist with the 'Irish Independent'.

His first novel, *Land without Stars*, was published in 1946, and from 1951 to 1964 Kiely was the literary editor of the 'Irish Press'. In 1964 Kiely resigned from full-time journalism to teach creative writing at several American universities. Benedict Kiely's writing is informed with a humanism and sense of history that is expressed in his most powerful novels, which were written as a response to the deepening sectarianism and violence of the Troubles in Northern Ireland, *Proxopera* and *Nothing Happens in Carmincross*.

In 1981 Kiely was a founding member of Aosdána, an association of Ireland's major artists, and in 1996 he was elected Saoi of Aosdána, the highest honour an Irish writer can receive. Benedict Kiely died in 2007.

His work continues to be celebrated at the annual Benedict Kiely Literary Weekend held in his native Omagh.

ALSO BY BENEDICT KIELY

Novels

Land Without Stars
In A Harbour Green
Call for a Miracle
Honey Seems Bitter
The Cards of the Gambler
There Was an Ancient
House
Dogs Enjoy the Morning
Proxopera
Nothing Happens in
Carmincross

Non-Fiction

Counties of Contention
Modern Irish Fiction
All the Way to Bantry
Bay – and Other Irish
Journeys
Poor Scholar: A Life of
William Carleton
And As I Rode by Granard
Moat
Drink to the Bird
Ireland from the Air
The Waves Behind Us

Short Stories

A Journey to the Seven
Streams
A Ball of Malt and
Madame Butterfly
A Cow in the House
A Letter to Peachtree

As editor

Yeats' Ireland
The Small Oxford Book of
Dublin
Penguin Book of Irish
Short Stories

Children's

The Trout in the Turnhole

Down Then By Derry

THREE STORIES

Benedict Kiely

Leabharlanna Poiblí Chathair Baile Átha Cliath
Dublin City Public Libraries

turnpike
books

'A Ball of Malt and Madame Butterfly' first appeared in
The Kenyon Review and 'Down Then By Derry' first appeared
in *The Dublin Review*; both were first collected in
A Ball of Malt and Madame Butterfly
(Victor Gollancz, 1973).

'The Fairy Women of Lisbellaw' first appeared in
The Journal of Irish Literature and was first collected in
A Cow in the House (Victor Gollancz, 1978)

This edition published 2019 by Turnpike Books

turnpikebooks@gmail.com

ISBN 9780993591372

Typeset in Plantin by MRules

Printed and bound by
Clays Ltd, Elcograf S.p.A.

CONTENTS

CONTENTS

A BALL OF MALT AND
MADAME BUTTERFLY

On a warm but not sunny June afternoon on a crowded Dublin street, by no means one of the city's most elegant streets, a small hotel, a sort of bed-and-breakfast place, went on fire. There was pandemonium at first, more panic than curiosity in the crowd. It was a street of decayed Georgian houses, high and narrow, with steep wooden staircases, and cluttered small shops on the ground floors: all great nourishment for flames. The fire, though, didn't turn out to be serious. The brigade easily contained and controlled it. The panic passed, gave way to curiosity, then to indignation and finally, alas, to laughter about the odd thing that had happened when the alarm was at its worse.

This was it.

From a window on the top-most floor a woman, scantily-clad, puts her head out and waves a patchwork bed coverlet, and screams for help. The stairway, she cries, is thick with smoke, herself and her husband are afraid to face it. On what would seem to be prompting from inside the room, she calls down that they are a honeymoon couple up from the country. That would account fairly enough for their still being abed on a warm June afternoon.

The customary ullagone and ullalu goes up from the crowd. The fire-engine ladder is aimed up to the window. A fireman begins to run up the ladder. Then suddenly the groom appears in shirt and trousers, and barefooted. For, to the horror of the beholders, he makes his bare feet visible by pushing the bride back into the room, clambering first out of the window, down the ladder like a monkey although he is a fairly corpulent man; with monkey-like agility dodging round the ascending fireman, then disappearing through the crowd. The people, indignant enough to trounce him, are still too concerned with the plight of the bride, and too astounded to seize him. The fireman ascends to the nuptial casement, helps the lady through the window and down the ladder, gallantly offering his jacket which covers some of her. Then when they are halfways down, the fireman, to the amazement of all, is seen to be laughing right merrily, the bride vituperating. But before they reach the ground she also is laughing. She is brunette, tall, but almost Japanese in appearance, and very handsome. A voice says: If she's a bride I can see no confetti in her hair.

She has fine legs which the fireman's jacket does nothing to conceal and which she takes pride, clearly, in displaying. She is a young woman of questionable virginity and well known to the fireman. She is the toast of a certain section of the town to whom she is affectionately known as Madame Butterfly, although unlike her more famous namesake she has never been married, nor cursed by an uncle bonze for violating the laws of the gods of her ancestors. She has another, registered, name: her mother's name. What she is her mother was before her, and proud of it.

The bare-footed fugitive was not, of course, a bridegroom, but a long-established married man with his wife and family and a prosperous business in Longford, the meanest town in Ireland. For the fun of it the firemen made certain that the news of his escapade in the June afternoon got back to Longford. They were fond of, even proud of, Butterfly as were many other men who had nothing at all to do with the quenching of fire.

But one man loved the pilgrim soul in her and his name was Pike Hunter.

Like Borgnefesse, the buccaneer of St. Malo on the Rance, who had a buttock shot or sliced off in action on the Spanish Main, Pike Hunter had a lopsided appearance when sitting down. Standing up he was as straight and well-balanced as a man could be: a higher civil servant approaching the age of forty, a shy bachelor, reared, nourished and guarded all his life by a trinity of upper-middle-class aunts. He was pink-faced, with a little fair hair left to emphasise early baldness, mild in his ways, with a slight stutter, somewhat afraid of women. He wore always dark-brown suits with a faint red stripe, dark-brown hats, rimless spectacles, shiny square-toed brown hand-made shoes with a wide welt. In summer, even on the hottest day, he carried a raincoat folded over his arm, and a rolled umbrella. When it rained he unfolded and wore the raincoat and opened and raised the umbrella. He suffered mildly from hay fever. In winter he belted himself into a heavy brown overcoat and wore galoshes. Nobody ever had such stiff white shirts. He favoured brown neckties distinguished with a pearl-headed pin. Why he sagged to one side, just a little to the left, when he sat down, I never knew. He had never been sliced or shot on the Spanish Main.

But the chance of a sunny still Sunday afternoon in Stephen's Green and Grafton Street, the select heart or soul of the city's south side, made a changed man out of him.

He had walked at his ease through the Green, taking the sun gratefully, blushing when he walked between the rows of young ladies lying back in deck-chairs. He blushed for two reasons: they were reclining, he was walking; they were as gracefully at rest as the swans on the lake, he was awkwardly in motion, conscious that his knees rose too high, that his sparse hair – because of the warmth he had his hat in his hand – danced long and ludicrously in the little wind, that his shoes squeaked. He was fearful that his right toe might kick his left heel, or vice versa, and that he would fall down and be laughed at in laughter like the sound of silver bells. He was also alarmingly aware of the bronze knees, and more than knees, that the young ladies exposed as they leaned back and relaxed in their light summer frocks. He would honestly have liked to stop and enumerate those knees, make an inventory – he was in the Department of Statistics; perhaps pat a few here and there. But the fearful regimen of that trinity of aunts forbade him even to glance sideways, and he stumbled on like a winkered horse, demented by the flashing to right and to left of bursting globes of bronze light.

Then on the park pathway before him, walking towards the main gate and the top of Grafton Street, he saw the poet. He had seen him before, but only in the Abbey Theatre and never on the street. Indeed it seemed hardly credible to Pike Hunter that such a man would walk on the common street where all ordinary or lesser men were free to place their feet. In the Abbey Theatre the poet had all the strut and style of a man who could walk with the gods, the Greek gods that is, not the gods in the theatre's cheapest seats. His custom was to enter by a small stairway, at the front of the house and in full view of the audience, a few moments before the lights dimmed and the famous gong sounded and the curtain rose. He walked slowly, hands clasped behind his back, definitely balancing the prone brow oppressive with its mind, the eagle head aloft and crested with foaming white hair. He would stand, his back to the curtain and facing the house. The chatter would cease, the fiddlers in the orchestra would saw with diminished fury. Some of the city wits said that what the poet really did at those times was to count the empty seats in the house and make a rapid reckoning of the night's takings. But their gibe could not diminish the majesty of those entrances, the majesty of the stance of the man. And there he was now, hands behind back, noble head high, pacing slowly, beginning the course of Grafton Street. Pike Hunter walked behind him, suiting his pace to the poet's, to the easy deliberate rhythms of the early love poetry: I would that we were, my beloved, white birds on the foam of the sea. There is a queen in China or, maybe, it's in Spain.

They walked between the opulent windows of elegant glittering shops, doors closed for Sunday. The sunshine had drawn the people from the streets: to the park, to the lush green country, to the seaside. Of the few people they did meet, not all of them seemed to know the poet was, but those who did know saluted quietly, with a modest and unaffected reverence, and one young man with a pretty girl on his arm stepped off the pavement, looked after the poet and clearly whispered to the maiden who it was that had just passed by the way. Stepping behind him at a respectful distance Pike felt like an acolyte behind a celebrant and regretted that there was no cope or cloak of cloth of gold to which he could humbly carry the train.

So they sailed north towards the Liffey, leaving Trinity College, with Burke standing haughty-headed and Goldsmith sipping at his honeypot of a book, to the right, and the Bank and Grattan orating Esto Perpetua, to the left, and Thomas Moore of the Melodies, brown, stooped and shabby, to the right; and came into Westmoreland Street where the wonder happened. For there approaching them came the woman Homer sung: old and grey and, perhaps, full of sleep, a face much and deeply lined and haggard, eyes sunken, yet still the face of the queen she had been when she and the poet were young and they had stood on the cliffs on Howth Head, high above the promontory that bears the Bailey Lighthouse as a warning torch and looks like the end of the world; and they had watched the soaring of the gulls and he had wished that he and she were only white birds, my beloved, buoyed out on the foam of the sea. She was very tall. She was not white, but all black in widow's weeds for the man she had married when she wouldn't marry the poet. Her black hat had a wide brim and, from the brim, an old-fashioned veil hung down before her face. The pilgrim soul in you, and loved the sorrows of your changing face.

Pike stood still, fearing that in a dream he had intruded on some holy place. The poet and the woman moved dreamlike towards each other, then stood still, not speaking, not saluting, at opposite street corners where Fleet Street comes narrowly from the East to join Westmoreland Street. Then still not speaking, not saluting, they turned into Fleet Street. When Pike tiptoed to the corner and peered around he saw that they had walked on opposite sides of the street for, perhaps, thirty paces, then turned at right angles, moved towards each other, stopped to talk in the middle of the street where a shaft of sunlight had defied the tall overshadowed buildings. Apart from themselves and Pike that portion of the town seemed to be awesomely empty; and there Pike left them and walked in a daze by the side of the Liffey to a pub called The Dark Cow. Something odd had happened to him: poetry, a vision of love?

*

It so happened that on that day Butterfly was in the Dark Cow, as, indeed, she often was: just Butterfly and Pike, and Jody with the red carbuncled face who owned the place and was genuinely kind to the girls of the town, and a few honest dockers who didn't count because they had money only for their own porter and were moral men, loyal to wives or sweethearts. It wasn't the sort of place Pike frequented. He had never seen Butterfly before: those odd slanting eyes, the glistening high-piled black hair, the well-defined bud of a mouth, the crossed legs, the knees that outclassed to the point of mockery all the bronze globes in Stephen's Green. Coming on top of his vision of the poet and the woman, all this was too much for him, driving him to a reckless courage that would have flabbergasted the three aunts. He leaned on the counter. She sat in an alcove that was a sort of throne for her, where on busier days she sat surrounded by her sorority. So he says to Jody whom he did not yet know as Jody: May I have the favour of buying the lady in the corner a drink?

That you may, and more besides.

— Please ask her permission. We must do these things properly.

— Oh there's a proper way of doing everything, even screwing a goose.

But Jody, messenger of love, walks to the alcove and formally asks the lady would she drink if the gentleman at the counter sends it over. She will. She will also allow him to join her. She whispers: Has he any money?

— Loaded, says Jody.

— Send him over so. Sunday's a dull day.

Pike sits down stiffly, leaning a little away from her, which seems to her quite right for him as she has already decided that he's a shy sort of man, upper class, but shy, not like some. He excuses himself from intruding. She says: You're not inthrudin'.

He says he hasn't the privilege of knowing her name.

Talks like a book, she decides, or a play in the Gaiety.

— Buttherfly, she says.

— Butterfly, he says, is a lovely name.

— Me Mother's name was Trixie, she volunteers.

— Was she dark like you?

— Oh, a natural blonde and very busty, well developed, you know. She danced in the old Tivoli where the newspaper office is now. I'm neat, not busty.

To his confusion she indicates, with hands moving in small curves, the parts of her that she considers are neat. But he notices that she has shapely long-fingered hands and he remembers that the poet had admitted that the small hands of his beloved were not, in fact, beautiful. He is very perturbed.

— Neat, she says, and well-made. Austin McDonnell, the fire-brigade chief, says that he read in a book that the best sizes and shapes would fit into champagne glasses.

He did wonder a little that a fire-brigade chief should be a quotable authority on female sizes and shapes, and on champagne glasses. But then and there he decided to buy her champagne, the only drink fit for such a queen who seemed as if she came, if not from China, at any rate from Japan.

— Champagne, he said.

— Bubbly, she said. I love bubbly.

Jody dusted the shoulders of the bottle that was on his shelves had waited a long time for a customer. He unwired the cork. The cork and the fizz shot up to the ceiling.

— This, she said, is my lucky day.

— The divine Bernhardt, said Pike, had a bath in champagne presented to her by a group of gentlemen who admired her.

— Water, she said, is better for washing.

But she told him that her mother who knew everything about actresses had told her that story, and told her that when, afterwards, the gentlemen bottled the contents of the bath and drank it, they had one bottleful too many. He was too far gone in fizz and love's frenzy to feel embarrassed. She was his discovery, his oriental queen.

He said: You're very oriental in appearance. You could be from Japan.

She said: My father was, they say. A sailor. Sailors come and go.

She giggled. She said: That's a joke. Come and go. Do you see it?

Pike saw it. He giggled with her. He was a doomed man.

She said: Austin McDonnell says that if I was in Japan I could be a geisha girl if I wasn't so tall. That's why they call me Buttherfly. It's the saddest story. Poor Madame Buttherfly died that her child could be happy across the sea. She married a sailor, too, an American lieutenant. They come and go. The priest, her uncle, cursed her for marrying a Yank.

— The priests are good at that, said Pike who, because

of his reading allowed himself, outside office hours, a soupcon of anticlericalism.

Touched by Puccini they were silent for a while, sipping champagne. With every sip Pike realised more clearly that he had found what the poet, another poet, an English one, had called the long-waited long-expected spring, he knew his heart had found a time to sing, the strength to soar was in his spirit's wing, that life was full of a triumphant sound and death could only be a little thing. She was good on the nose, too. She was wise in the ways of perfume. The skin of her neck had a pearly glow. The three guardian aunts were as far away as the moon. Then one of the pub's two doors – it was a corner house – opened with a crash and a big man came in, well drunk, very jovial. He wore a wide-brimmed grey hat. He walked to the counter. He said: Jody, old bootlegger, old friend of mine, old friend of Al Capone, serve me a drink to sober me up.

— Austin, said Jody, what will it be?

— A ball of malt, the big man said, and Madame Butterfly.

— That's my friend, Austin, she said, he always says that for a joke.

Pike, whose face, with love or champagne or indignation, was taut and hot all over, said that he didn't think it was much of a joke.

— Oh, for Janey's sake, Pike, be your age.

She used his first name for the first time. His eyes were moist.

— For Janey's sake, it's a joke. He's a father to me. He knew my mother.

— He's not Japanese.

— Mind your manners. He's a fireman.

— Austin, she called. Champagne. Pike Hunter's buying Champagne.

Pike bought another bottle, while Austin towered above them, swept the wide-brimmed hat from his head in a cavalier half-circle, dropped it on the head of Jody whose red carbuncled face was thus half-extinguished. Butterfly giggled. She said: Austin, you're a scream. He knew Trixie, Pike. He knew Trixie when she was the queen of the boards in the old Tivoli.

Sitting down, the big man sang in a ringing tenor: For I knew Trixie when Trixie was a child.

He sipped at his ball of malt. He sipped at a glass of Pike's champagne. He said: It's a great day for the Irish. It's a great day to break a fiver. Butterfly, dear girl, we fixed the Longford lout. He'll never leave Longford again. The wife has him tethered and spancelled in the haggard. We wrote poison-pen letters to half the town, including the parish priest.

— I never doubted ye, she said. Leave it to the firemen, I said.

— The Dublin Fire Brigade, Austin said, has as long an arm as the Irish Republican Army.

— Austin, she told Pike, died for Ireland.

He sipped champagne. He sipped whiskey. He said: Not once, but several times. When it was neither popular or profitable. By the living God, we was there when we was wanted. Volunteer McDonnell, at your service.

His bald head shone and showed freckles. His

startlingly blue eyes were brightened and dilated by booze. He said: Did I know Trixie, light on her feet as the foam on the fountain? Come in and see the horses. That's what we used to say to the girls when I was a young fireman. Genuine horsepower the fire-engines ran on then, and the harness hung on hooks ready to drop on the horses as the firemen descended the greasy pole. And where the horses were, the hay and the straw were plentiful enough to make couches for Cleopatra. That was why we asked the girls in to see the horses. The sailors from the ships, homeless men all, had no such comforts and conveniences. They used to envy us, Butterfly, my geisha girl, you should have been alive then. We'd have shown you the jumps.

Pike was affronted. He was almost prepared to say so and take the consequences. But Butterfly stole his thunder. She stood up, kissed the jovial big man smack on the bald head and then, as light on her feet as her mother could have been, danced up and down the floor, tight hips bouncing, fingers clicking, singing: I'm the smartest little geisha in Japan, in Japan. And the people call me Rolee Polee Nan, Polee Nan.

Drowning in desire, Pike forgot his indignation and found that he was liking the man who could provoke such an exhibition. Breathless, she sat down again, suddenly kissed Pike on the cheek, said: I love you too. I love champagne. Let's have another bottle.

They had.

— Rolee Polee Nan, she sang as the cork and fizz ascended.

— A great writer, a Russian, Pike said, wrote that his ideal was to be idle and to make love to a plump girl.

— The cheek of him. I'm not plump. Turkeys are plump. I love being tall, with long legs.

Displaying the agility of a trained high-kicker with hinges in her hips she, still sitting, raised her shapely right leg, up and up as if her toes would touch the ceiling, up and up until stocking-top, suspender, bare thigh and a frill of pink panties, showed. Something happened to Pike that had nothing at all to do with poetry or Jody's champagne. He held Butterfly's hand. She made a cat's cradle with their fingers and swung the locked hands pendulum-wise. She sang: Janey Mac, the child's a black, what will we do on Sunday? Put him to bed and cover his head and don't let him up until Monday.

Austin had momentarily absented himself for gentlemanly reasons. From the basement jakes his voice singing rose above the soft inland murmur of falling water: Oh my boat can lightly float in the heel of wind and weather, and outrace the smartest hooker between Galway and Kinsale.

The dockers methodically drank their pints of black porter and paid no attention. Jody said: Time's money. Why don't the two of you slip upstairs. Your heads would make a lovely pair on a pillow.

Austin was singing: Oh she's neat, oh she's sweet, she's a beauty every line, the Queen of Connemara is that bounding barque of mine.

He was so shy, Butterfly said afterwards, that he might have been a Christian Brother and a young one at that, although where and how she ever got the experience to enable her to make the comparison, or why she should think an old Christian Brother less cuthallacht than a young one, she didn't say. He told her all about the aunts and the odd way he had been reared and she, naturally, told Austin and Jody and all her sorority. But they were a kind people and no mockers, and Pike never knew, Austin told me, that Jody's clientele listened with such absorbed interest to the story of his life, and of his heart and his love-making. He was something new in their experience, and Jody's stable of girls had experienced a lot, and Austin a lot more, and Jody more than the whole shebang, and all the fire-brigade, put together.

For Jody, Austin told me, had made the price of the Dark Cow in a basement in Chicago. During the prohibition, as they called it, although what they prohibited it would be hard to say. He was one of five brothers from the bogs of Manulla in the middle of nowhere in the County of Mayo. The five of them emigrated to Chicago. When Al Capone and his merry men discovered that Jody and his brothers had the real true secret about how to make booze, and to make it good, down they went into the cellar and didn't see daylight nor breathe fresh air, except to surface to go to Mass on Sundays, until they left the U.S.A. They made a fair fortune. At least four of them did. The fifth was murdered.

Jody was a bachelor man and he was good to the girls. He took his pleasures with them as a gentleman might, with the natural result that he was poxed to the eyebrows. But he was worth more to them than the money he quite generously paid after every turn or trick on the rumpled, always

unmade bed in the two-storeyed apartment above the pub.
He was a kind uncle to them. He gave them a friendly welcome, a place to sit down, free drink and smokes and loans,
or advances for services yet to be rendered, when they were
down on their luck. He had the ear of the civic guards and
could help a girl when she was in trouble. He paid fines
when they were unavoidable, and bills when they could no
longer be postponed, and had an aunt who was reverend
mother in a home for unmarried mothers and who was,
like her nephew, a kindly person. Now and again, like the
Madame made famous by Maupassant, he took a bevy or
flock of the girls for a day at the seaside or in the country.
A friend of mine and myself, travelling into the granite
mountains south of the city, to the old stone-cutters' villages of Lackan and Ballyknockan where there were aged
people who had never seen Dublin, thirty miles away,
and never wanted to, came upon a most delightful scene
in the old country pub in Lackan. All around the bench
around the walls sat the mountainy men, the stone-cutters,
drinking their pints. But the floor was in possession of a
score of wild girls, all dancing together, resting off and on
for more drink, laughing, happy, their gaiety inspired and
directed by one man in the middle of the floor: red-faced,
carbuncled, oily black hair sleeked down and parted up
the middle in the style of Dixie Dean, the famous soccer
centre-forward, whom Jody so much admired. All the
drinks were on generous Jody.

So in Jody's friendly house Pike had, as he came close
to forty years, what he never had in the cold abode of the
three aunts: a home with a father, Austin, and a brother,

Jody, and any God's amount of sisters; and Butterfly who, to judge by the tales she told afterwards, was a motherly sort of lover to him and, for a while, a sympathetic listener. For a while, only: because nothing in her birth, background, rearing or education, had equipped her to listen to so much poetry and talk about poetry.

— Poor Pike, she'd say, he'd puke you with poethry. Poethry's all very well, but.

She had never worked out what came after that qualifying: But.

— Give us a bar of a song, Austin. There's some sense to singing. But poethry. My heart leaps up when I behold a rainbow in the sky. On Linden when the sun was low. The lady of Shalott left the room to go to the pot. Janey preserve us from poethry.

He has eyes, Jody told Austin and myself, for no girl except Butterfly. Reckon, in one way, we can't blame him for that. She sure is the smartest filly showing in this paddock. But there must be moderation in all things. Big Anne, now, isn't bad, nor her sister, both well-built Sligo girls and very co-operative, nor Joany Maher from Waterford, nor Patty Daley from Castleisland in the County Kerry who married the Limey in Brum but left him when she found he was as queer as a three-dollar bill. And what about little Red Annie Byrne from Kilkenny City, very attractive if it just wasn't for the teeth she lost when the cattleman that claimed he caught gonorrhoea from her gave her an unmerciful hammering in Cumberland Street. We got him before he left town. We cured more than his gonorrhoea.

— But, Austin said, when following your advice, Jody, and against my own better judgement, I tried to explain all that to Pike, what does he do but quote to me what the playboy of the Abbey Theatre, John M. Synge, wrote in a love poem about counting queens in Glenmacnass in the Wicklow mountains.

— In the Wicklow mountains, said Jody. Queens? With the smell of the bog and the peat smoke off them.

Austin, a great man, ever, to sing at the top of his tenor voice about Dark Rosaleen and the Queen of Connemara and the County of Mayo, was a literary class of a fireman. That was one reason why Pike and himself got on so well together, in spite of that initial momentary misunderstanding about the ball of malt and Madame Butterfly.

— Seven dog days, Austin said, the playboy said he let pass, he and his girl, counting Queens in Glenmacnass. The queens he mentions, Jody, you never saw, even in Chicago.

— Never saw daylight in Chicago.

— The Queen of Sheba, Austin said, and Helen, and Maeve the warrior queen of Connacht, and Deirdre of the Sorrows and Gloriana that was the great Elizabeth of England and Judith out of the Bible that chopped the block of Holofernes.

— All, said Jody, in a wet glen in Wicklow. A likely bloody story.

— There was one queen in the poem that had an amber belly.

— Jaundice, said Jody. Or Butterfly herself that's as sallow as any Jap. Austin, you're a worst lunatic than Pike.

— But in the end, Jody, his own girl was the queen of all queens. They were dead and rotten. She was alive.

— Not much of a compliment to her, Jody said, to prefer her to a cartload of corpses.

— Love's love, Jody. Even the girls admit that. They've no grudge against him for seeing nobody but Butterfly.

— They give him a fool's pardon. But no doll in the hustling game, Austin, can afford to spend all her time listening to poetry. Besides, girls like a variety of pricks. Butterfly's no better or worse than the next. When Pike finds that out he'll go crazy. If he isn't crazy already.

That was the day, I recall, that Butterfly came in wearing the fancy fur coat – just a little out of season. Jody had, for some reason or other, given her a five-pound note. Pike knew nothing about that. And Jody told her to venture the five pounds on a horse that was running at the Curragh of Kildare, that a man in Kilcullen on the edge of the Curragh had told him that the jockey's wife had already bought her ball dress for the victory celebration. The Kilcullen man knew his onions, and his jockeys, and shared his wisdom only with a select few so as to keep the odds at a good twenty to one.

— She's gone out to the bookie's, said Jody, to pick up her winnings. We'll have a party tonight.

Jody had a tenner on the beast.

— She could invest it, said Austin, if she was wise. The day will come when her looks will go.

— Pike might propose to her, said Jody. He's mad enough for anything.

— The aunts might devour him. And her.

— Here she comes, Jody said. She invested her winnings on her fancy back.

She had too, and well she carried them in the shape of pale or silver musquash, and three of her sorority walked behind her like ladies-in-waiting behind the Queen of England. There was a party in which even the dockers joined, but not Pike, for that evening and night one of his aunt's was at death's door in a nursing home, and Pike and the other two aunts were by her side. He wasn't to see the musquash until he took Butterfly for an outing to the romantic hill of Howth where the poet and the woman had seen the white birds. That was the last day Pike ever took Butterfly anywhere. The aunt recovered. They were a thrawn hardy trio.

Pike had become a devotee. Every day except Sunday he lunched in Jody's, on a sandwich of stale bread and leathery ham and a glass of beer, just on the off-chance that Butterfly might be out of the doss and abroad, and in Jody's, at that, to her, unseasonable hour of the day. She seldom was, except when she was deplorably short of money. In the better eating places on Grafton Street and Stephen's Green, his colleagues absorbed the meals that enabled higher civil servants to face up to the afternoon and the responsibilities of State: statistics, land commission, local government, posts and telegraphs, internal revenue. He had never, among his own kind, been much of a mixer: so that few of his peers even noticed the speed with which, when at five in the evening the official day was done, he took himself, and his hat and coat and umbrella, and legged it off to Jody's: in the hope that Butterfly might be there, bathed and perfumed and ready for wine and love. Sometimes she was. Sometimes she wasn't. She liked Pike. She didn't deny it. She was always an honest girl, as her mother, Trixie, had been before her – so Austin said when he remembered Trixie who died in a hurry, of peritonitis. But, Janey Mac, Butterfly couldn't have Pike Hunter for breakfast, dinner, tea and supper, and nibblers as well, all the livelong day and night. She still, as Jody said, had her first million to make, and Pike's inordinate attachment was coming between her and the real big business, as when, say, the country cattle men were in town for the market. They were the men who knew how to get rid of the money.

— There is this big cattle man, she tells Austin once, big he is in every way, who never knows or cares what he's spending. He's a gift and a godsend to the girls. He gets so drunk that all you have to do to humour him is play with him a little in the taxi going from pub to pub and see that he gets safely to his hotel. The taximen are on to the game and get their divvy out of the loot.

One wet and windy night, it seems, Butterfly and this philanthropist are flying high together, he on brandy, she on champagne, for which that first encounter with Pike has given her a ferocious drouth. In the back of the taxi touring from pub to pub, the five pound notes are flowing out of your man like water out of a pressed sponge. Butterfly is picking them up and stuffing them into her handbag, but not all of them. For this is too good and too big for any taximan on a fair percentage basis. So for every one note she puts into her handbag she stuffs two or three down into the calf-length boots she is wearing against the wet weather. She knows, you see, that she is too far gone in bubbly to walk up the stairs to her own room, that the tax-iman, decent fellow, will help her up and then, fair enough, go through her bag and take his cut. Which, indeed, in due time he does. When she wakes up, fully clothed, in the morning on her own bed, and pulls off her boots, her ankles, what with the rain that had dribbled down into her boots, are poultice and plastered with notes of the banks of Ireland and of England, and one moreover of the Bank of Bonnie Scotland.

— Rings on my fingers, she says, and bells on my toes.

That was the gallant life that Pike's constant attendance was cutting her off from. She also hated being owned. She hated other people thinking that she was owned. She hated like hell when Pike would enter the Dark Cow and one of the other girls or, worse still, another man, a bit of variety, would move away from her side to let Pike take the throne. They weren't married, for Janey's sake. She could have hated Pike, except that she was as tender-hearted as Trixie had been, and she liked champagne. She certainly felt at liberty to hate the three aunts who made a mollycoddle out of him. She also hated, with a hatred that grew and grew, the way that Piked puked her with poethry. And all this time poor Pike walked in a dream that he never defined for us, perhaps not even for himself, but that certainly must have looked higher than the occasional trick on Jody's rumpled bed. So dreaming, sleep-walking, he persuaded Butterfly to go to Howth Head with him one dull hot day when the town was empty and she had nothing better to do. No place could have been more fatally poetic than Howth. She wore her musquash. Not even the heat could part her from it.

— He never let up, she said, not once from the moment we boarded the bus on the quays. Poethry. I had my bellyful.

— Sure thing, said Jody.

— Any man, she said, that won't pay every time he performs is a man to keep a cautious eye on. Not that he's not generous. But at the wrong times. Money down or no play's my motto.

— Well I know that, said Jody.

— But Pike Hunter says that would make our love mercenary, whatever that is.

— You're a great girl, said Austin, to be able to pronounce it.

— Your middle name, said Jody, is mercenary.

— My middle name, thank you, is Imelda. And the cheek of Pike Hunter suggesting to me to go to a doctor because he noticed something wrong with himself, a kidney disorder, he said. He must wet the bed.

— Butterfly, said Austin, he might have been giving you good advice.

— Nevertheless. It's not for him to say.

When they saw from the bus the Bull Wall holding the northern sand back from clogging up the harbour, and the Bull Island, three miles long, with dunes, bent grass, golfers, bathers and skylarks, Pike told her about some fellow called Joyce – there was a Joyce in the Civic

Guards, a Galwayman who played county football, but
no relation – who had gone walking on the Island one fine
day and laid eyes on a young one, wading in a pool, with
her skirts well pulled up; and let a roar out of him. By all
accounts this Joyce was no addition to the family for, as
Pike told the story, Butterfly worked out that the young
one was well under age.

Pike and Butterfly had lunch by the edge of the sea, in
the Claremount Hotel, and that was all right. Then they
walked in the grounds of Howth Castle, Pike had a special pass and the flowers and shrubs were a sight to see if
only Pike had kept his mouth shut about some limey by
the name of Spenser who landed there in the year of God,
and wrote a poem as long as from here to Killarney about
a fairy queen and a gentle knight who was pricking on the
plain like the members of the Harp Cycling Club, Junior
Branch, up above there in the Phoenix Park. He didn't
get time to finish the poem, the poet that is, not Pike, for
the Cork people burned him out of house and home and,
as far as Butterfly was concerned, that was the only good
deed she ever heard attributed to the Cork people.

The Phoenix Park and the Harp Club reminded her
that one day Jody had said, meaning no harm, about the
way Pike moped around the Dark Cow when Butterfly
wasn't there, that Pike was the victim of a semi-horn and
should go up the Fifteen Acres and put it in the grass for
a while and run around it. But when, for fun, she told this
to Pike he got so huffed he didn't speak for half an hour,
and they walked Howth Head until her feet were blistered
and the heel of her right shoe broke, and the sweat, with

the weight of the musquash and the heat of the day, was running between her shoulders-blades like a cloudburst down the gutter. Then the row and the ructions, as the song says, soon began. He said she should have worn flat-heeled shoes. She said that if she had known that he was conscripting her for a forced march over a mountain she'd have borrowed a pair of boots from the last soldier she gave it to at cut-price, for the soldiers, God help them, didn't have much money but they were more open-handed with what they had than some people who had plenty, and soldiers didn't waste time and breath on poetry: Be you fat or be you lean there is no soap like Preservene.

So she sat on the summit of Howth and looked at the lighthouse and the seagulls, while Pike walked back to the village to have the broken heel mended, and the sweat dried cold on her, and she was perished. Then when he came back, off he was again about how that white-headed old character that you'd see across the river there at the Abbey Theatre, and Madame Gone Mad McBride that was the age of ninety and looked it, and known to all as a roaring rebel, worse than Austin, had stood there on that very spot, and how the poet wrote a poem wishing for himself and herself to be turned into seagulls, the big dirty brutes that you'd see along the docks robbing the pigeons of their food. Butterfly would have laughed at him, except that her teeth by this time were tap-dancing with the cold like the twinkling feet of Fred Astaire. So she pulled her coat around her and said: Pike, I'm no seagull. For Janey's sake take me back to civilisation and Jody's where I know someone.

But, God sees, you never knew nobody, for at that moment the caveman came out in Pike Hunter, he that was always so backward on Jody's bed and, there and then, he tried to flatten her in the heather in the full view of all Dublin and the coast of Ireland as far south as Wicklow Head and as far north as where the Mountains of Mourne sweep down to the sea.

— Oh none of that, Pike Hunter, she says, my good musquash will be crucified. There's a time and a place and a price for everything.

You and your musquash, he tells her.

They were wrestling like Man Mountain Dean and Jack Doyle, the Gorgeous Gael.

— You've neither sense nor taste, says he, to be wearing a fur coat on a day like this.

— Bloody well for you to talk, says she, with your rolled umbrella and your woollen combinations and your wobbly ass that won't keep you straight in the chair, and your three witches of maiden aunts never touched, tasted or handled by mortal man, and plenty of money and everything your own way. This is my only coat that's decent, in case you haven't noticed, and I earned it hard and honest with Jody, a generous man but a monster on the bed, I bled after him.

That put a stop to the wrestling. He brought her back to the Dark Cow and left her at the door and went his way.

He never came back to the Dark Cow but once, and Butterfly wasn't on her throne that night. It was the night before the cattle-market. He was so lugubrious and woe-begone that Jody and Austin and a few merry newspaper men, including myself, tried to jolly him up, take him out of himself by making jokes at his expense that would force him to come alive and answer back. Our efforts failed. He looked at us sadly and said: Boys, Beethoven, when he was dying, said: Clap now, good friends, the comedy is done.

He was more than a little drunk and, for the first time, seemed lopsided when standing up; and untidy.

— Clap now indeed, said Jody.

Pike departed and never returned. He took to steady drinking in places like the Shelbourne Hotel or the Buttery in the Hibernian where it was most unlikely, even with Dublin being the democratic sort of town that it is, that he would ever encounter Madame Butterfly. He became a great problem for his colleagues and his superior officers in the civil service, and for his three aunts. After careful consultation they, all together, persuaded him to rest up in Saint Patrick's Hospital where, as you all may remember, Dean Swift died roaring. Which was, I feel sure, why Pike wasn't there to pay the last respects to the dead when Jody dropped from a heart attack and was waked in the bedroom above the Dark Cow. The girls were there in force to say an eternal farewell to a good friend. Since the drink was plentiful and the fun and the mourning intense, somebody, not even Austin knew who, suggested that the part of the corpse that the girls knew best should be tastefully decorated with black crepe ribbon. The honour of tying on the ribbon naturally went to Madame Butterfly but it was Big Anne who burst into tears and cried out: Jody's dead and gone forever.

Austin met her, Butterfly not Big Anne, a few days

afterwards at the foot of the Nelson Pillar. Jody's successor had routed the girls from the Dark Cow. Austin told her about Pike and where he was. She brooded a bit. She said it was a pity, but nobody could do nothing for him, that those three aunts had spoiled him for ever and, anyway, didn't Austin think that he was a bit astray in the head.

— Who knows, Butterfly? Who's sound or who's silly? Consider yourself for a moment.

— What about me, Austin?

— A lovely girl like you, a vision from the romantic east, and think of the life you lead. It can have no good ending. Let me tell you a story, Butterfly. There was a girl once in London, a slavey, a poor domestic servant. I knew a redcoat here in the old British days who said he preferred slaveys to anything else because they were clean, free and flattering.

— Austin, I was never a slavey.

— No Butterfly, you have your proper pride. But listen: this slavey is out one morning scrubbing the stone steps in front of the big house she works in, bucket and brush, carbolic soap and all that, in one of the great squares in one of the more classy parts of London Town. There she is on her bended knees when a gentleman walks past, a British army major in the Coldstream Guards or the Black Watch or something.

— I've heard of them, Austin.

— So this British major looks at her, and he sees the naked backs of her legs, thighs you know, and taps her on the shoulder or somewhere and he says: Oh, rise up, lovely maiden and come along with me, there's a better life in store for you somewhere else. She left the bucket and the brush, and the stone steps half-scrubbed, and walked off with him and became his girl. But there were even greater things in store for her. For, Butterfly, that slavey became Lady Emma Hamilton, the beloved of Lord Nelson, the greatest British sailor that ever sailed, and the victor of the renowned battle of Trafalgar. There he is up on the top of the Pillar.

— You wouldn't think to look at him, Austin, that he had much love in him.

— But, Butterfly, meditate on that story, and rise up and get yourself out of the gutter. You're handsome enough to be the second Lady Hamilton.

After that remark, Austin brought her into Lloyd's, a famous house of worship in North Earl Street under the shadow of Lord Nelson and his pillar. In Lloyd's he bought her a drink and out of the kindness of his great singing heart, gave her some money. She shook his hand and said: Austin, you're the nicest man I ever met.

Austin had, we may suppose, given her an image, an ideal. She may have been wearied by Pike and his sad attachment to poetry, but she rose to the glimmering vision of herself as a great lady beloved by a great and valiant lord. A year later she married a docker, a decent quiet hard-working fellow who had slowly sipped his pints of black porter and watched and waited all the time.

Oddly enough, Austin told me when the dignity of old age had gathered around him like the glow of corn-stubble in the afterwards of harvest.

He could still sing. His voice never grew old.

— Oddly enough, I never had anything to do with her. That way, I mean. Well you know me. Fine wife, splendid sons, nobody like them in the world. Fine daughters, too. But a cousin of mine, a ship's wireless operator who had been all round the world from Yukohama to the Belgian Congo and back again, and had had a ship burned under him in Bermuda and, for good value, another ship burned under him in Belfast, said she was the meanest whore he ever met. When he had paid her the stated price, there were some coppers left in his hand and she grabbed them and said: give us these for the gas-meter.

But he said, also, that at the high moments she had a curious and diverting way of raising and bending and extending her left leg – not her right leg which she kept as flat as a plumb-level. He had never encountered the like before, in any colour or in any country.

THE FAIRY WOMEN
OF LISBELLAW

If it hadn't been for an elderly blonde that I saw sitting in the sun in a bikini on a lawn in Atlanta, Georgia, I'd never have remembered him again. She was a good 40 paces away from me as I stepped out with two friends from the door of my yellow-brick apartment building. Her back was towards us. She was the only object that disturbed the green grass, and very green it was to grow up out of the red clay of the dry sunny south.

She swivelled her head, left to right, and looked around at us. Although I didn't know who she was and had never even seen her before or, at any rate, had never seen that much of her, I waved my right hand. For beyond her, although in reality there was nothing but the street called Ponce de Leon where it ceases to be suburbia and becomes a stretch of rooming-houses and heavy traffic, and black girls washing cars, and a good Greek restaurant on the far side of the traffic, I saw clearly the

Atlantic rolling in on the cliffs of Donegal, and the dark rocks of Roguey under which only the most courageous ever venture to swim.

So Gene asked me who the blonde on the grass was and I said I didn't know.

— But you waved at her.

— Wouldn't you wave at any girl in a bikini?

— A girl, Dolores said.

— I waved at the past.

— You sure did, Gene said. She's 90. You crazy Irish.

— We're a friendly people, I said.

We walked away from the aged blonde towards the car-park at the back of the apartments.

I gave up trying to be a Jesuit in the second year of the novitiate, not because of my vocation, as we called it, had weakened – I gravely doubt if I'd ever heard a voice calling me anywhere – but because I had a broken back. Well, it wasn't exactly broken the way you'd snap a twig. It was a spinal lesion, an injured spot on which the bacillus that lurks in all of us settled to make it difficult for me to bend if I was straight or to straighten up if I was bent, and to make me feel that some unseen demon stabbed now and again, slowly and carefully, with a thin red-hot knitting-needle about the region of the third lumbar lump. Eighteen months of Christian patience it took to exorcise that demon.

The Atlantic breakers, white and blue and green, and flashing a lot of colours I could put no name to, came trampling and tumbling up Bundoran strand. The surf was crowded with happy shouting bathers. Little children, grave with excitement, rode slowly on tiny brown hairy donkeys, and one enterprising entertainer had even introduced a baby elephant. The hurdy-gurdy at the hobby-horses and chairaplanes was squeezing the last drop of melody out of the tune that went to the words about the old rustic bridge by the mill:

'Twas oftimes, dear Maggie, when years passed
    away,
And we plighted lovers became ...

The town was a long thin line along the coast behind me as I left the red strand and climbed the steep short-grassed slope to the top of the cliffs above Roguey Rocks. Golfers, like jerky clockwork toys, moved, bent with no pain, drove with the intensity of cyclones, on the windy links around Bundoran's grandest hotel. That wind was strong and salty. Behind the town the flat-topped mountains, all the way from Rossinver Braes to bare Ben Bulben, lay like sleeping purple animals. The straps that held my back-splint in place were cutting into my armpits and crotch. My shiny black jacket, that had fitted well enough when I went into hospital eighteen months previously, had a hard job now to keep buttoned because of the back-splint and a slight stomach spread developed in hospital. In that place of rolling ocean and salt shouting wind, purple mountains, hurdy-gurdies and near-naked bathers, I was, and felt I was, a cheerless sombre figure.

This clifftop walk was my path of escape. It brought

me away from the happy all-together crowds that seemed so nastily to emphasize my own isolated predicament. Beyond Roguey the cliffs – flung spray rising high above them, high as they were, and spattering the rocks – swung directly eastwards and so, unavoidably did the path. It brought me by the bowl-shaped fresh-water spring, clear as crystal against solid rock, that was one of the wonders of those cliffs. It brought me by an even more wonderful wonder, the Fairy Bridges, where the sea had moled its way through weaknesses in the dark rock and, far back from the dangerous slanting edge of the cliffs, you could look down into deep terrifying cauldrons of boiling froth. Tragedies were always happening there: daring young people clambering down the sides of the cauldrons, to what purpose God alone knew, and losing foothold or handhold, and falling down where not all the lifeguards in the world could be of the least assistance to them.

Beyond those fatal Fairy Bridges the holiday crowd had vanished. There was an odd courting couple, snug from the wind behind a fence of green sods or a drystone wall, grazing nimble goats who sometimes attacked people; and inland, protected by the cliffs by walls and fences, easy grazing cattle. The great flat mountains were still visible, but the eye and imagination were taken now by the long rising-and-falling range of highlands far across the bay.

Poems had been written about this place, that vision of highlands, strand and sea, and far away the estuary of the River Erne. The strand was perilous with quicksands and so generally deserted.

From Dooran to the Fairy Bridge
And down by Tullan Strand,
Level and long and white with waves,
Where gull and curlew stand ...

The wooden shelter that I sat and read in was as near to being my own exclusive property as made no difference. It was roofed with red tiles, and had no sides, and a cruciform wooden partition held up the roof and divided the structure into four parts so that no matter from what airt the wind did blow, myself and my book always had shelter. There I sat reading, day-dreaming, I was nineteen, remembering. Remembering now and again the Jesuit novitiate where, inexplicably, I had been happy in a brief fit of religious frenzy that was to be my ration ever since. A classical rectangular house that had once belonged to a great lord and, with red carpet on the main avenue, given welcome to an English king, sheltered in deep pine woods in the sleepy Irish midlands. Bells divided the holy day. Black-gowned neophytes made their meditations, walked modestly, talked circumspectly. Wood pigeons cooed continuously, and there were more bluebells and daffodils and red squirrels in those woods that I have ever seen anywhere else in the world.

But, to be honest, I was never quite sure what I was doing there and, if I was happy, it was happiness in a sort of trance that I felt uneasily must have its end. My lumbar spine made up my mind for me, and eighteen months surrounded by fresh and pleasant young Irish nurses convinced me that there were certain things that Jesuits were not normally supposed to have. So that my memories in the cruciform shelter were less about the Ignatian spiritual exercises than about dreams of fair women in blue-and-white uniforms. They were all there, around the corner by Ben Bulben and off through Sligo on the high road to Dublin. To the rocks and the seawind I repeated the names of the seven or eight of them I had fallen in love with: Lane, Devlin, Brady, Love, Callaghan, Mullarkey, O'Shea, Rush and Moynihan. On a recount: nine.

Far away a black-sailed boat that seemed scarcely to be moving came down the sand-channel of the Erne estuary to the sea. In the privacy of the shelter I eased the crotch-straps of the back-splint. It was made of good leather stretched on a light steel frame, it travelled from the neck to the buttocks, it smelled of horse-harness.

— Head out to sea, I said, when on your lee the breakers you discern. Adieu to all the billowy coasts and the winding banks of Erne.

The tide, the bathers, the children, the donkeys, and even the baby elephant, had withdrawn for a while from the red half-moon of Bundoran Strand. Far out the frustrated breakers were less boisterous. The hurdy-gurdy was silent and the hobby-horses resting at their stalls, and in hotels and boarding-houses the evening meal was being demolished. In Miss Kerrigan's old-fashioned whitewashed Lios na Mara, or the Fort, God help us, by the sea, my mother looked up from her ham salad to say that I was late as usual.

— Sara Alice, leave him be, Miss Kerrigan said. He's

thinking long. Waiting for the happy day when he gets back to his studies. Looking forward to his ordination, God bless him, the holy oil, the power to bind and loose.

Listening to her I kept my thoughts fixed on red squirrels flashing in bluebell woods, on the wasps' nest at the foot of the Spanish chestnut tree close to the croquet court, on the dark silent file of neophytes, eyes cast down, obeying the holy bell and walking to the chapel to morning oblation – along cold corridors and down a stairway up which unholy royalty had once staggered to bed. For I felt if my thoughts were on laughing young nurses, Lane, Devlin, Brady, Love, Callaghan, Mullarkey, O'Shea, Rush and Moynihan, my nine blue-and-white Muses, Miss Kerrigan's sharp brown eyes would discover those thoughts and betray the old Adam hiding behind the shiny black suit.

— Thinking long, she said again.

She was very fond of me and I wouldn't have hurt her for the world. Lios na Mara, too, was a place that caught the fancy as the average seaside boarding-house most certainly did not. It stood well back from the town's one interminable street, under a stone archway, secure and secluded in a grassy courtyard that overlooked the toy harbour where the fishing-boats and the seagulls were. It wasn't New York, or Liverpool but it was the first harbour I ever saw and, as a child, I had actually thought that the ships might sail from that harbour to anywhere or Antananarivo.

— This, said Miss Kerrigan, is Master McAtavey.

He had come into the room silently while, with my back to the door, I was fumbling with a napkin and sitting

down to attack my ham. It was a surprise to find anyone
except my mother and Miss Kerrigan, who were girlhood
friends, and myself, of course, by right of inheritance, in
that small private parlour. The other guests ate elsewhere
and did not presume.

— My only sister's son, said Miss Kerrigan.

— From the Glen of Glenties, said my mother who was
hell all out for geography.

He was still standing, very tall and awkward, three
paces away from the table.

— Sit down, Eunan dear, said my mother. Don't be shy.

She disliked shy people. She suspected them of
dishonesty.

— He teaches school, said Miss Kerrigan.

— In the Vale of Dibbin, said my mother. A heavenly
place. You know it, she said to me.

Then he blushed. Never before or since have I seen a
blush like it. He had fair curly hair that was cropped too
short and his eyes were a startlingly bright and childish
blue. His navy-blue pinstripe was too short in the sleeves
and, above strong square hands, the knobs on his wrists
were as large as golfballs. He had taken two paces forward abruptly as if he were a sentry under command,
towards his provender, so that the lower half of him was
hidden by the table and I couldn't see whether the legs of
his pants, like his sleeves, were too short. Not that I, with
my shiny coat of clerical black, straining to meet around
my back-splint, was in any position to criticize. His blond
skin - once it must have been blond – was so beaten by the
heathery wind of the Glen of Glenties, and burned by the

same sun that shines both on Glenties and Georgia, that even experts on the matter would have considered it quite impossible for him to blush.

But he did. The blush went upwards in little leaps or spurts, an inch or so at a time, from the tight white collar that squeezed his long neck, up and up, spreading, intensifying until his whole face shone, as the man said about the sunset, like a forge. He was a very shy master and let me say, to my credit, that I leaped up, offered him a chair, seated him at his ham salad, sat down again and talked non-stop for half an hour about the Vale of Dibbin and the Glen of Glenties. He choked over his ham, and played back to me the occasional yes or no, and I wasn't sure whether he was grateful or resentful. But I didn't care much, for I did know the places I talked about and to talk about them was a pleasure in itself.

The town of Glenties, I told them, was always bright with paint and so spotlessly clean that a scrap of paper or cigarette butt wasn't to be seen on the street, and a bluebottle fly, invading from some less-regulated town, wouldn't last for five minutes. A few miles away, the sands, under clear water where the Gweebarra River turned salt, shone like silver. In the Vale of Dibbin the neat white-washed farmhouses stood along the breast of the mountain and the clean fields sloped steeply down to a trout stream, all white cataracts and deep populated pools. On which river I had fished with my brother and a fat man called Joe Maguire who had fought at the Dardanelles and who wore a bowler hat even when he was fishing.

The life and times of Joe Maguire could have kept me

going for half a day, but time was passing and I prized the private hours ahead when I would sit in my room and read and look down on the harbour and across the water at the happy company on the strand. They couldn't see me but I could see them and that, in some way or other, helped my morale. When I stopped to draw breath and chew ham I was glad to see that his blush had faded.

Miss Kerrigan listened, and watched me with loving brown eyes that were set deeply in a long wrinkled yellow face. She continuously rubbed her feet on the floor in a nervous way she had. That nervousness increased when she went to whist-drives and it was said that once, when she was running hard for first prize, she had rubbed a hole in the uncarpeted floor of the cardroom in a parish hall in a neighbouring town. She always dressed in black, in mourning for her father and mother who had died within the one week 30 years ago, and she was six feet two inches in height.

— What a memory, she said.

— A powerful man to tell stories, said my mother, like his father before him.

— A blessed gift, Miss Kerrigan said, and will stand to him well after ordination.

She must have meant something else, for no one could have suspected Miss Kerrigan of anti-clericalism.

— In the pulpit I mean, she said.

That didn't make it any better.

— I'll go for a walk now, said Eunan McAtavey.

Those were the first words I'd heard him say. They began as a whispering squeak and then spread out like a shout. They had clearly cost him premeditation and effort.

He stood up. He didn't overturn his chair. He did drop his napkin. I picked it up for him.

— Bernard will go with you, Miss Kerrigan said.

— Bernard, my mother said, Eunan was never here before. He doesn't know his way around.

There went my private hours, but politeness compelled me and, at any rate, the ladies had me trapped.

Three lovely old ladies lived in that block of yellow-brick apartments. Taken all-together they were a sort of sign that something remained in a place where everything was rapidly changing.

They lived in a world of their own and had memories that had nothing whatsoever to do with their neighbours. Forty years ago, when they had come to live there, those apartments had been new and quite the thing. But suburbia in automobiles had swept far beyond them. The district decayed. The old ladies stayed on because they were too old, perhaps too poor, to move. Their neighbours now were myself, and the withered blonde whoever she was, and rowdy students who had lively parties and were occasionally evicted because the landlord would find six living in an apartment he had rented to two. To evict one such group his workmen had to take the door off the hinges. A few decent quiet linotype men lived there. The paper they had worked for in a more southern city had folded and they had come north to Atlanta to find work. A flock of go-go girls who were working down the street stayed for a while, brightened the lawn with bodies more naked than had ever startled Eunan McAtavey on Bundoran Strand, then flew off elsewhere. Their place was taken one evening by a fat oily bald man. From their windows the students made offensive noises. Two burglars who lived in another part of the city rented one of the yellow apartments to keep their loot in. The police came and were a whole afternoon carrying out and counting miscellaneous objects. My next-door neighbour was a girl from Nashville who was married at fifteen and whose husband dressed up as the tiger in the tank at a filling-station. He walked out every morning in his costume, his own head showing, the tiger's head grinning in his hand.

Gene drove down the slope. We passed the hotel where the black girl, coming to fill her fifth date for the night, had changed her mind and tried to steal the cash register instead, and had been shot dead by the night porter. We passed three liquor stores, an army induction centre, a Sears Roebuck, a waste-patch that had once been a ball-park and would, any day henceforth, sprout skyscrapers. The twenty black girls washing cars were, to keep cool, squirting water over each other. We passed a Yarab shrine, a Presbyterian centre, a motel, three churches, a pop place painted all purple, saloons, and shops, and one skyscraper hotel at the corner of Peachtree Street. Dolores was on the way to a suburban shopping centre to buy shoes.

That was the first of seven walks, dull enough, silence mostly between us, our chief activities just walking, or tossing driftwood back into the tide, or simply sitting and gazing out to sea. He couldn't swim and I, because of my third lumbar lump and my back-splint, wasn't allowed to.

Now and again, to break the silence, I played courier and pointed out the estuary, named the mountains and quoted the poetry. He showed no interest. He would walk stolidly beside me, and I had a crazy feeling that his arms swung together, both before him at the same time, both behind him at the same time, if you know what I mean. The pinstripe trousers were, indeed, too short, and the feet were considerable. When he put away the pinstripe – he said it was his Sunday best and the salt air faded dark cloth – and put on grey flannels with a dangerous crease, they also were too short. His oatmeal tweed jacket creaked from the shop and my back-splint answered. We were a fine pair to be seen on any gay promenade. He never nonchalantly put his hands in his pockets. When he stood up they hung by his side as if he had no control over them.

On the fifth walk I talked about the Jesuits and the novitiate and the weedy lake where boating and bathing were allowed, depending on the weather, on major Christian festivals. He responded by telling me, in broken spurts and mumbles, how he had spent two years of hell in a teachers' training college in Dublin, and that he might as well, for all the college ever taught him about life, have been incarcerated, he used that word, in Mountjoy Jail. That reference to life should have warned me.

On the sixth walk I mentioned the nurses and litanied the nine magic names and, growing reckless with wishful thinking, hinted at nights of love under dimmed lights. On the seventh walk he stopped in the sunshine, on a path through the dunes beyond Tullan Strand, and raised his stiff right arm to indicate the curves and hollows of the dry sand, the sleek comfort of the bent grass, and said hoarsely: This would be a bloody great place to have a woman.

— True enough, I said and felt guilty before his awkward innocent passion.

For by day in the shelter when the crotch straps were eased, by night in bed when my black garments were laid aside, I had skipped in fantasy up and down those same dunes, a satyr in pursuit of nine nymphs, or lurked in grassy corners to cut off unclad stragglers.

— The way you talk about the place I come from, he said, you'd think it was Blackpool or the Land of Youth.

It took me until the following day to appreciate the juxtaposition but, on reflection in the quietude of my room, it seemed reasonable. The poets don't tell us, but there must have been beaches and bathing beauties in the land to which Niamh led Oisin. Eunan, clearly, had given the matter long thought.

— It's lovely country, I said. A home for poets. The fishing's good.

— I don't fish. The only poetry I ever learned off by heart was this.

He stood up stiff as a guardsman, filled his lungs with seawind and let fly: Bracing breezes, silvery sands, booming breakers, lovely lands. Come to Bundoran.

It didn't occur to me, I remember, to be surprised at this display of eloquence. Being talkative myself, I must have assumed that there was as much talk in everyone, that it was welling up in him and that some day the dam would burst.

— I learned that out of an advertisement in the newspaper

because it was my intention to come here to Bundoran for the women. I'd heard time and again that the place was hoaching with them during the Scottish holiday season.

Hoaching was a word we used to describe the way fingerling fish, in low water and warm weather, would swarm together at the mouths of pools. It was an evocative sultry word.

— What's holding you up? I said. They're everywhere to be seen.

Even in the lonely dunes that was true. Couples sprawled in sheltered corners. When they couldn't be seen they could be heard: muffled voices, and shrills of laughter quickly stifled, to remind the horseman passing by that love was all. The path we followed skirted the barbed wire of a military camp, went down a slope past an ancient churchyard to join the main road to Ballyshannon, Enniskillen, Omagh and Donegal town. Four green soldiers stood where the path joined the roadway and bantered and jackacted with six girls with bright flaring skirts and Glasgow accents.

— A surplus of two, he said. The soldiers have all the luck. You were lucky, too, with all those nurses. You struck it lucky. All good things. They say the nurses are the best. They know everything.

If I had not already come close to believing that my own imaginings were reality I might have had an attack of conscience for all the tall tales I had told him.

— My trouble, Bernard, is that I can't talk to women. Even your mother and Miss Kerrigan frighten me. I never had the training. Where would I get it? With mountainy women as wild as the mountain sheep? Hands on them as hard as flagstones. I never got a bloody chance. Even in Dublin. The priests in the college wouldn't let you see daylight. The Vincentians.

— No, I said, I suppose the Vincentians wouldn't be so good at that. It wouldn't be on the curriculum.

It worried me a little that he didn't laugh at the idea. He looked straight in front of him. His mouth, and it was a small tight one for such a large man, was tightly closed – now that his talking was over for the moment. Muscle stood out on the point of his left jaw as if he had his teeth clenched on his grievance. The hard sidewalk, crowded with women, I suppose there must have been men there too, was hot under our feet, the long town ahead. He had touchingly used my name for the first time and so made me his ally, his sworn brother sweet, his voice when it came to putting chat on the women.

He was so awkward on his feet that he came into the class of men who can be described as getting in their own way. Walking beside him had all sorts of problems. It wasn't so bad when he was silent, as he seldom was after he had confessed to me his true reason for coming to Bundoran. For when he was silent he could follow a straight course as well as any man. But when he talked he moved, inch by inch as his blush did, sideways in little spurts towards his listener, and to emphasize his point he jabbed with his elbows. Or they did the jabbing all on their own, for of all the men I've known, he had the least control over his hands and elbows and feet. To make his feet more noticeable he purchased and wore a pair of those rubber-and-corduroy pampooties known to the civilized world as brothel creepers. They didn't go with the iron crease of his grey flannels nor the creaking jacket of honest oatmeal tweed. They were also too big for him, although that seemed impossible, but the toes certainly flopped when he walked or stumbled along sideways, elbowing, so that every 50 yards or so I had to dodge to the other side of him to save myself from bruises and correct our course. We were the rarest-looking pair of Romeos that ever walked out to rummage and ruin the girls, Scottish or Irish, that hoached in that summery pool.

— You're a man of the world, he said. You can talk to people.

Nobody had ever said that to me before. Nobody has ever said it since, although two months later, as a student in Dublin walking home by night, I picked up a little girl with a blue beret and a brown belted coat and protruding teeth, and kissed her good-night at her garden gate. She breathed deeply. She said: Boy, you've got technique.

Afterwards the risks I took with more sophisticated college lasses, to establish my claim to a technique which until then I had been quite innocent, must have earned me an odd sort of reputation. But breathing bracing breezes, walking silvery sands, listening to, because I was unable to plunge into, booming breakers, it was up to me, as a man of the world, to do something for my hapless mountainy man. It wasn't going to be easy.

— Not that one, Bernard. She's as bold as brass by the cut of her.

— Isn't that what we're after, Eunan?

— She would talk the ass out of a pot. And the laughs of her.

The plump girl in orange swimsuit and blue bathing-cap ran, leaping and laughing, into the surf. Her thin blonde companion, in red suit and no cap, trotted demurely behind her, squeaking a little now and again. Little did the plump girl know how close she had come to the arms of Eunan McAtavey. He looked after her for a long time. He fancied her but he was afraid of her laughter.

— Not that one, Bernard. You couldn't get near her for lipstick.

This was a tall redhead, long flying red hair, who went round and round riding sidesaddle and flashing thighs on the hobby-horses. Her crimson mouth was, indeed, a size larger than nature, but only a man who had more on hand than he could deal with, could have faulted her for that. For a man who had nothing at all, nor ever had, Eunan of the Glen was mighty choosy. He feared laughter. He feared lipstick. He didn't want to spend money.

— Not that one, Bernard. She's a chain-smoker. Look at the burns on the ground around her. A bank manager couldn't keep her in cigarettes.

The thin girl in dark slacks and dark woollen sweater sat on a bench outside the Hamilton Hotel and blew out smoke as if she meant to blind the passers-by. She was gone beyond her first bloom but there was something appealingly wistful, and promising, about her dark steady eyes, and cheeks that hollowed as she sucked smoke.

— Not that pair, Bernard. They remind me of the mountainy girls at home.

They were sisters, two country girls, bright red berets, damp tails of hair straggling out from under the berets, belted fawn raincoats. Like ourselves and a hundred others, they had raced for shelter from an Atlantic squall to play the machines in hurdy-gurdy country. They stamped with delight in the deep churned discoloured sand. For fun, they shouldered each other like county footballers while they both grabbed for the one arm of the one-armed bandit. They laughed so as to be heard above the noise of a crowd of people crushed suddenly into a small space, even above the steam-organ hurdy-gurdy noises. The hobby-horses, all mounted, circled, the redhead sidesaddle. The rising-and-falling mountain range beyond the bay was hidden by a pitch-black cloud that came down like a smothering curtain. Then the curtain was split by forked lightning and the thunder came before the flash had faded. Under the wooden roof of the place of hobby-horses and bandits it was then so dark that one of the showmen switched on the lights. More lightning, the thunder seemed to come closer. A woman screamed and more children than you could count or kill began to cry. The elder of the two laughing sisters turned round and looked at us, and began to laugh as if she had just learned the secret. No question or doubt about it, nor was there any point in mentioning the matter to Eunan – but she was laughing at us.

Dolores is a slender sensitive woman who paints well and exhibits and sells her paintings. Gene, in spite of an English surname, has Arab blood in him that makes him look like a non-aggressive, even affable, slightly smaller

version of General Nasser. On Saturday afternoons Rich's
in Lennox Square in Atlanta, Georgia, is as good a field
as I've ever seen for the wholehearted bird-watcher. Gene
and Dolores couldn't see him, but Eunan of the Glen, lost
to me long ago by the Donegal sea, was beside me on the
escalator on the way up to the shoe department. He was
so real to me that day, for the first time in 27 years, that
I was ready to speak to him out loud, ready to hear him
say: No, Bernard, not that one. She couldn't be a modest
girl. Look at the bare back of her. Be the holy, if the parish
priest saw the like of that on a teacher's wife in the Glen
of Glenties, there'd be a new teacher in the school before
the end of the month if not sooner.

Yet Eunan – it must have been something he read –
had desired, I think, silks and perfumes with the sins he
imagined and feared: and the silks and perfumes were
all here. It was the women of his own mountainy place
and people that he feared most. He told me of a girl who
grabbed his hand in the darkness of the schoolhouse at a
travelling movie show: She had a palm, Bernard, as hard
as a whinstone rock. It would frighten you. A woman
shouldn't be like that. A woman should be gentle. And
true. Terrible things, Bernard, can happen to country
schoolmasters. A man I heard tell of got into trouble with
the girls in the school, two of them, and one was jealous
of the other, and she told. The country girls are deceitful.
And if you married the wrong one your job's ruined.

Looking up the escalator at the bare-backed beauty
ahead of us, I said that you could play the zither on the
knuckles of her spine.

She was a tall olive Amazonian, with her right shoulder arrogantly bare, and white pants so tight that her bottom looked like an outsize meringue; and a crimson waistcoat all front and no back, that was a miracle of cantilever.

But it was Gene, not Eunan, that heard. Bundoran was 27 years away, and 4,000 miles.

— Hardly worth while, he said, for her escort to take her home. Nothing more left to see. Billy Graham says that it's okay for girls to wear miniskirts if there is no intention of provoking sensual desire.

Oh Eunan McAtavey where are you now?

Failure after failure, he wouldn't take the jump, so there was nothing for it now but the Palais de Danse. As a man I know says: If you want to get it you must go where it is.

Miss Kerrigan would say to me: You're more cheerful now, Bernard, since Eunan came. You're not thinking long any more. I'm so glad the two of you get along together. Good healthy walks, bracing breezes, silvery sands.

Everybody in the bloody place seemed to know the jingle off by heart.

— Booming breakers, lovely lands, rhymed my mother.

— That's real poetry, she said smugly and just to madden me for she knew that I kept hidden in my room above the harbour the steadily accumulating collected works: three developing epics, one on Barc, Deborah and King Sisera in the *Book of Judges*, one on the Easter Rising of 1916, one on the lightning by St Patrick, on the Hill of Slane, of Ireland's first-ever Pascal fire. Apart of course, from many shorter pieces of an intense lyricism, inspired

by one or other or all of the chosen nine: Could I into that
silent shrine advance, to where the sacred flame makes all
things plain, what joy were mine to find engraven there
my name.

— Good healthy walks, said Miss Kerrigan. But don't
overdo it. Think of your back and all that lying down and
standing up for ordination.

She was right: I mean about the thinking long. For I
had now an interest in life outside myself, and was more
anxious that Eunan should find his woman, and find
engraven there his name, than he was himself. He had
nothing: my hoard or pocket of nine nurses was in Dublin
beyond the mountains, I could afford to be generous. For
to be afflicted by desire for hoaching Scottish lasses, and
yet not be able to say a blessed preliminary word to any
one of them must have been pain beyond pain. Once in
a while he would whisper, spluttering sideways into my
ear, gripping my bicep hard enough to hurt, as if he were
trying to hold himself back from leaping on the lady there
and then: That one, Bernard. That's the ticket. God, it
would be something to give her a run for it in the sandhills.

Nearly always the desired one was pale, golden-haired,
prim, modestly dressed and an obvious member of the
Children of Mary. This puzzled me for a while until I
realized sadly that Eunan, perhaps subconsciously, was
attracted to young women whose appearance would please
the parish priest. When I managed to put chat on one of
these votaresses Eunan was no help at all: arms dangling,
mouth like a vice, gaze at a tangent – towards the breakers,
or the bulk of Truskmore concealing Ben Bulben, or the

cliffs of Slieve League across the bay. So there was nothing for it but the Palais de Danse where not even a shy buck like Eunan would have a chance of escape, for far and wide the place was notorious for frenzied women. Even the boom-thump-boom-thump-boom of it, echoing night after night from the sea to the hills and back again was the cause of protests and letters to the local paper.

— See it, Eunan, you must. If you went back to Glenties and said you'd never seen the inside of the palais they'd laugh at you. They'd do worse. They'd worry about you.

The palais also had the name for being a rough class of a place. There was a long-nosed man I knew from my own town, who kept the entire works of Edgar Wallace in a tin trunk under his bed, and had got mildly drunk one night in the palais and had bones broken by the gorillas. Not a word of this did I tell to Eunan, he was nervous enough as it was, nor was I all that happy myself: shiny tight black suit and creaking back-splint smelling like horse-harness weren't exactly standard equipment for the palais. What would I say to the first girl who put her arm around me to convince her that I wasn't made of leather or wood, or about to perish with a petrifying disease?

We crossed the strand. A mist-swollen moon was coming up slowly from behind Truskmore. The surf shone, the cliff-shadows were jet-black on the sand, the small stream that dribbled across the strand was silver. The glaring lights, the boom-thump-boom of the palais were sacrilege. Restive Eunan at any moment might turn and bolt like a colt running from harness and, if he did, I'd have no power to halt him. For now that I was face-to-face with the palais I was damned near as nervous as he was, and not much more of a man of the world. Nearer and nearer. The entering crowd shuffled around a doorway guarded by the two gorillas who had beaten up the long-nosed devotee of Edgar Wallace. The lights were blinding, the noise deafening. Eunan was moving more slowly, had, indeed, almost come to a halt, when a woman's voice said clearly into my ear: Is it going to say Mass you are, your reverence? Or has somebody had a sudden heart-attack?

It was the laughing girl. She was still laughing. So was her sister. They were linked, and leaning against each other with unaffected gaiety.

— It's no place for a clerical student, the elder sister said.

— An ex-clerical student.

— A clerical error, then.

They laughed fit to fall at the ancient joke and I couldn't but laugh with them, while Eunan stood there as stiff as my back-splint.

— There was a fight in there already, she said.

The younger sister, as I recall, never spoke, but only laughed.

— Drunken animals. The civic guards took away two that you couldn't see for blood.

She took my arm: Let's go for a walk to Tullaghan. There's a lovely moon.

Tullaghan was two miles to the side of the town away from the Fairy Bridges and my four-cornered wooden shelter. A concrete pathway led along the tops of low cliffs, the sea to the right, quiet residential hotels to the left.

Beyond the rock bathing-pool that was reserved for nuns the hotels ended and there was nothing but grass, grey-white under the moon, and the moon shining on the water.

— I'm Ellen, she said. That there behind is Madge, my sister. We'd be twins only she's two years younger.

Behind us in the salty moonlight Madge was laughing gently but continuously, Eunan wasn't making even a grunt, and it was a wonder to God to me that he had come walking at all: except to escape from the more certain horrors of the palais.

— She's very like you. Except that she laughs more.

— We both laugh a lot. But Madge laughs more because she's shy.

— She's in proper company this blessed night.

— He does look shy, too. Where's he from?

— The hills of Donegal.

— All night and day I'm dreaming, she sang, of the hills of Donegal.

Then she said: we're from the meadows of Fermanagh, from Lisbellaw.

Lisbellaw I knew, as I knew then the half of Ireland: Lisbellaw, and the sleepy lake shore and grass meadows all around. The map shows us a filigree pattern of blue, Upper Lough Erne, on a field of flat green: restful country, quiet towns, little harbours with long names where you could idle away ten life-times fishing spoon or spinning minnow for pike and perch and bream. It made me warm to her right away that she came from a countryside meant for laziness or, since I was literary then, lotus-eating. She swung easily on my arm, and sometimes went one, two, three and a one, two, three on the tips of her toes as if she were readying to dance the Walls of Limerick. So I slipped my arms around her waist and felt like the hell of an ex-cleric, and hoped I was giving good example to Eunan lumbering along behind us.

She was wearing a green sort of dress, not a raincoat as when she had first surfaced in the place of the one-armed bandits. She had a small golden-coloured harp as a clasp at the cleavage, no beret, her dark hair dry and shampoo-shiny, and held in place by a golden-coloured snood; nor did she smell of peat smoke as it was generally said that rural beauties did. Thus, we came to the old square tower that guards the eel-weir at Bundrowes, where the Drowes, which is a magic river, meets the sea, and all the wonder of Tullaghan Strand was before us: no ordinary level of sand where people went bathing, but rank upon rank of oval stones that the sea had shaped. They shone, between salt and moonshine, like gigantic jewels. All along the country roads out of Bundoran, into Donegal and Leitrim and Sligo, you could see Tullaghan stones painted all colours and making borders for beds in flower gardens.

Ellen and myself sat in the shadow of the tower and looked out on the flashing Drowes where the trout have the gizzards of chickens because of a miracle performed by a saint back there at Lough Melvin where the river comes from. She said that when she and Madge went back to Lisbellaw they'd take Tullaghan stones with them, and paint them striped, and keep them as souvenirs of this lovely night. That set us kissing and grappling merrily in the shadows. When we came up for air she asked: Where are they?

Oh, there they were, sure enough, not rolling on the grass or wrestling in the shadows but standing 50 yards from us on the bank of the Drowes, and five yards from each other: Eunan, a dark statue, arms by its side, that looked as if it had been there as long as the tower. They were too far away from us to hear if Madge was still laughing. Since there was nothing, short of roping them together that we could do about it, we kissed and grappled again and when we had surfaced again they were exactly as we had last seen them enchanted to stone by magic river and sea and moon. Ellen breathed a long breath and slowly let it loose again. She said: They'd never credit it in Lisbellaw.

— Ellen, I know a song about Lisbellaw.

— Sing it, for God's sake.

— It's in Irish.

— Sing it in Irish.

So I sang in Irish the verse that mentions Lisbellaw.

— What does it mean?

— Something like this: I met a fairy woman down at Lisbellaw and asked her would any key unlock the lock of love. In low and kind and gentle voice she answered me: When love locks the heart the lock will never be loosened.

— It would be grand, she said, but I doubt if it's true.

We kissed again, quietly and without grappling. She stood up and smoothed down the green dress and said we'd better walk home before Madge froze to death or leaped in the Drowes for lack of anything better to do.

The fighting was over for the night in the Palais de Danse. The long moonlit town, painted all colours for the

holiday season, was asleep, it seemed, and silent, except
that you could guess that here and there and everywhere
it was still a holiday and the fun was going on. We left
the sisters at the door of their boarding-house. Because
of Eunan, or rather because of Madge, I forbore kissing
Ellen good-night, but she understood, and gripped my
hand hard, and dug her nails into my palm, and said we'd
meet tomorrow night by the hobby-horses, and hoped that
the moon would be out again.

Eunan and myself walked wordless home along the
bright empty street. It wasn't until we were at Miss
Kerrigan's door that he spoke: Bernard, she had a very
hard hand.

I said nothing.

— That one, Bernard, was laughing at me all night.

— Not at you, Eunan. She was laughing because she's
young and on her holidays.

After a while I added: And walking out with a young
man by the bright silvery light of the moon.

— Bernard, ever since the first day I went to school
country girls have been laughing at me.

Up in my silent room I couldn't even read myself to
sleep, feeling sorrier then for lonely Eunan than out at
Tullaghan I had felt for laughing Madge.

The morn was breaking fresh and fair and the lark sang
in the sky, and it was as lovely a day as you would expect
after such a night of moonlight. Eunan and myself walked
like automatons across the strand. What, I asked myself,
are the wild waves saying, for Eunan hadn't a word to

throw to land or ocean, nor could I think of anything
to say that wouldn't make the poor man more miserable
than he obviously was already. In sad silence we came to
the two high flights of wooden steps that went up from
a moist cliff-shadowed corner of the strand to the top of
Roguey. Eunan climbed up ahead of me – as blithely as a
man climbing to the scaffold. He had his pinstripe on and
his trousers, God help me, seemed to have shrunk. Up
above us there was music and dancing and singing voices.
The local branch of the Gaelic League kept an open-air
dancing-floor at that point on the clifftop, and all day long,
Maryanne, weather permitting, the young people were at
it hammer and tongs: slip jig and hornpipe and fourteen-
hand reel, the Walls of Limerick, the Waves of Tory, Saddle
the Pony, the Mason's Apron and the Chaffpool Post. It
was such a lively place and such a beautiful morning. Far
out, wisps of mist drifted over dark-blue unbroken water.
There was autumn in the air. The flat-topped mountains
were still hidden. Because of the noise of the music and
dancing the cries from the strand were inaudible, so that
the silent movements of the people on the edge of the surf,
and of the donkeys and the baby elephant, seemed completely senseless. White mist, too, drifted in bundles over
the golf-links, and the clockwork figures stepping out of the
mist, vanishing into it again were crazily comic.

It was part of the mood of the morning that I should at
that moment see the blonde and purple woman, 50 yards
away, higher up the slope on the path to the Fairy Bridges.
She sat quite close to the cliff's edge. She waved and I
waved in return.

— Who is that? says Eunan.

— What we're after, Eunan. Scottish and glamorous. Look at that purple dress, that blonde hair.

The blonde hair shone in the morning. She waved again.

— That there's no laughing country girl, Eunan. Perfume, I'd say, that would flatten a regiment. If there was a wind this morning we'd get the perfume already.

Side-by-side, keeping step, we advanced up the slope. Behind us the dancing and music went on as if we never had been. His big feet beside me were no longer flopping in brothel creepers but solid and determined in square-toed black shoes. The woman was reading a book, her head turned away from us. At 60 paces it was clear that I had been right about the perfume.

— Good-morning, I said.

It was an irreproachable and perfectly accurate remark.

She turned her head and looked at us and said: To whom have I the honour of speaking?

It wasn't that she was old: remembering her now I suppose she couldn't have been more than 60. She wore red shoes and purple stockings, and her short purple dress, tucked up to allow her to squat in comfort, showed fat knees with pads of surplus flesh to the insides of the kneecaps. It wasn't that she was ugly. It was the desperate effort to defeat ugliness that made me feel that life could be a losing battle. She wore a loose purple jacket about as long as the dress, and a striped blouse – I can't remember the colour of the stripes – and a foamy sort of syllabubbly chiffon scarf emerging from the neckline of the dress, which was cut like a schoolgirl's gym-frock. That now was what she wore, for she was the sort of woman that you looked first at the radiant clothes before you came face to face with her face. On her left hand she seemed to wear two wedding rings and an engagement ring and a keeper. She had fine plump hands. But the face was a mask, with long false lashes and, below the eyes, radiating black streaks that looked as if they had been done with a sharp knife dipped in cobbler's dye. The eyes, which were not unkind, moved almost audibly when they moved at all. It wasn't that we were disappointed in her, it was my awful feeling that she too had her dreams and that the pair of us did not fulfil them.

Her voice, I will confess, was a little shrill and she had, in so far as I could judge, a Lancashire way of speaking, which is fine in its own way but you want to know English very well to keep up with it. To this day I can see her quite clearly, apart from the colours of the stripes in her blouse, and I remember her with interest and a great curiosity. I can even hear her talking – about her husband who was coming to Bundoran to join her. She was a fit rival for the mysterious Atlantic which was at that moment her background: oceans of women, all waiting for daring young mariners.

But Eunan, like Bishop Berkeley, thought otherwise. He was already ten yards away and moving fast while I was preparing to squat beside her, even though squatting in a back-splint was a trick that took some rehearsing.

— My husband, she said, had a special sort of tandem bicycle built all to his own specifications. We frequently take trips on it.

At least that's what I thought she said. But what between the Lancashire accent and the state of confusion in which

Eunan's retreat left me, I could have imagined the words: they didn't seem very likely. There he went, his arms stiff as logs, his trouser-bottoms halfways to his knees.

— What's wrong with your friend? she said. Was he short-taken?

She laughed fit to frighten the gulls and, since I couldn't think of anything to say and couldn't laugh with her, I fled. Her laughter followed me. My back-splint seemed to have slipped its moorings, but that also was imagination. Truskmore was pushing one jagged rocky shoulder out of the mist. Come and cover me, oh mist, hide me from that laughter, and hell run away with Eunan McAtavey who could at least have stood his ground until, with dignity, we retreated together. But when I came on him in the crowd by the dancing-floor he looked so hapless that I could find no word of reproach.

— An error of judgement, Eunan, I said. She looked all right from a distance.

— They all do.

The dancers were having the time of their lives. Nobody paid the least attention to us.

— That's the sort of woman, he said, that you're warned against in the catechism.

— You're from a different diocese, Eunan. The catechism where I came from never mentioned the likes of her.

— She was mentioned somewhere if it wasn't in the catechism.

We walked on by the freshwater spring and the Fairy Bridges and the four-cornered shelter in which, to my annoyance, there was a young couple holding hands and gazing out to sea: Head out to sea when on your lee the breakers you discern. Oh, adieu to all the billowy coasts.

We crossed Tullan Strand with its gulls and curlews, and crossed the sand-dunes and walked the long street to Lios na Mara and didn't swap a word all the way. Up in my room I opened my neglected books, took notebook and pencil and set to the reading: this was my business, I was a frost and failure as a man of the world and, as a pimp, quite preposterous. He was so silent at lunch and again at high tea, ham salad, that I knew Miss Kerrigan and my mother thought we had had a row, but were too polite to say anything about it; and that night there was no moon and no Eunan.

The morning mist had dissolved into mizzling rain. He hadn't even told Miss Kerrigan that he was going. Without any feeling in her voice my mother said: I hope you weren't rude to him. He was so shy.

The lights around the hurdy-gurdies were bleary weeping eyes. The hobby-horses, riderless, went round a few times, then halted hopelessly, and their music stopped and there was no sound between sea and the mountains but the boom-thump-boom of the palais. I wore a heavy black cloth coat and a black hat and looked, Ellen said, like a parish priest on the run. With a rain-coated girl on each arm I walked as far as the four-cornered shelter. The weather was telling us that the holidays were over and that everything came to an end.

— He ran away from us, Ellen said. He was afraid of the fairy women of Lisbellaw.

When I told them about the purple blonde on the clifftop they laughed for ten minutes, and went on laughing at the idea of Eunan, suitcase in hand, legging it back to the mountainy safety of the Vale of Dibbin. In the four-cornered shelter I profited by his absence and made gentle love to the two of them. Oh, it was all very harmless: running from one corner to another, grappling, kissing, with two girls who couldn't stop laughing; discovering that shy Madge was far and away the more ardent of the two. We walked back through rising wind that blew the clamour of the palais off towards Lough Melvin. The town was a long line of weeping lights. When we came as far as the hobby-horses, the music – although the animals were at rest – was playing about the old rustic bridge by the mill, and Ellen and Madge sang:

> But one day we parted in pain and regret,
> Our vows then we could not fulfil.

— Too true, Ellen said. We're off tomorrow.

— But you'll write, Madge said.

— And we'll meet again next year, Ellen said.

— Maybe, said Madge, you might come to see us in Lisbellaw.

Although I meant to write, I never did: Dublin and the nine, and other things, distracted me. The next year I wasn't in Bundoran; and although ten years later I passed briefly through Lisbellaw, there was another woman with me and I never even thought of Madge and Ellen. As I said, if it hadn't been for the ancient blonde on the green in Atlanta I'd never even have remembered Eunan.

*

A beautiful blonde girl sat in a chair and in the most queenly fashion allowed herself to be fitted with pink shoes. A serious youth, he couldn't have been more than eighteen, knelt at her feet and did the fitting. She was searching for a shoe of a colour that would match some detail in the dress she wore. Patiently the young fellow eased the dainty foot into shoe after shoe after shoe. We marvelled at his restraint.

— What, Gene said, is behind the American rape epidemic?

That had been a joke between us, not a very good one, ever since we had seen the question printed on the cover of a lurid magazine, and with it the picture of a man with billiard-ball eyes roping a buxom, and quite unconcerned, lady to a chair. We were still guessing at answers, and watching the young kneeling troubadour and the girl of the pink shoes, when Dolores returned. We drove back to my place. The aged blonde was gone from the green.

On that very day my mother was writing me a letter. That sort of coincidence is common. For instance, on a day in a college in Virginia when a student was asking me about a friend of mine, a singer, he, in Chicago, was mailing me his newest long-player.

My mother wrote:

Miss Kerrigan, whom you may recall, died recently and I went to Bundoran to the funeral. May she rest in peace. She was a dear woman, albeit a little eccentric, and thought the world and all of you,

and thought in her final doting days that you were
a priest and wondered why you never came to see
her. I always told her that you were far away on the
foreign missions and that the Jesuits were strict and
didn't allow you home often. It wasn't much of a
lie, and I feel that God and even the Jesuits would
forgive me. She prayed for you every night. But
who should be at the funeral only your companion
of long ago, Eunan McAtavey, with his wife and
nine children, a car-load of them. They seemed
very happy. He was asking for you. He said he read
everything you wrote, in newspapers and even in
books.

On what dusty lovely Donegal roadway, walking home
from school or Mass or market day shopping, did he, or
how did he, manage to tell a girl that he loved her?

They seemed very happy, she said. He was asking for
me. He had read everything I had written. Ah well, his
memory was better than mine. He couldn't very well
explain to my mother and his wife why he ran, or what he
ran, or thought he was running, from. What ever became,
I wonder, of the fairy women of Lisbellaw?

DOWN THEN BY DERRY

The first time Tom Cunningham ever saw Sadie Law's brother, Francie, that brother was airborne between the saddle of a racing bicycle and a stockade filled with female lunatics. Francie is not the chief part of this story, nor is his sister, but since he had been mentioned, it might be fair to his fame and memory to say who he was and what he was doing in the air in that odd place.

A resident medical officer in that district's mental hospital had, years before, been a believer in athletics as curative therapy for the crazy: running and jumping and the lord knows what. So he set those who were out of cells and strait-jackets, and otherwise capable, at the running and jumping, barring, for good reasons the throwing of the hammer or the discus, or the tossing of the caber – which can be dangerous occupations even for the sane. Then the medical officer, to introduce a sanative, competitive spirit, organised an annual sports meeting, with cups, shields and lesser prizes. The thing grew and grew. That medical officer died and went to Valhalla. The annual meeting continued to grow until it was one of the most notable sporting events in that part of the country. Professionals competed. The crazy men and women, those of them who could be out and about, were now only two small corralled sections among the spectators. They had been pushed back into the shouting or gibbering shadows where everybody, except the man in Valhalla, thought they belonged.

Francie Law was a famous track cyclist. That was how he came to be there in the air. There was one bad corner on the packed cinder track. This day there was a pile-up and Francie was catapulted clean, to land among the lunatic ladies. He survived. It was as a hero-worshipper bearing grapes to Francie's hospital bedside – Francie, wherever he was, always smelled of embrocation – that Tom Cunningham first met Francie's sister, Sadie, who was almost as famous as her brother, but not for track-cycling.

— She's Number One, according to all the talk, Tom said to his favourite friend who was five years younger than him.

Tom was nineteen.

— And she liked me, Tom said. We have a date. She wore a black leather coat with a belt. There was a good warm smell off it. Like the smell of the plush seats at the back of the cinema where all the feeling goes on. Hot stuff, boy. Also the smell of embrocation. Rub it up good. Frank Mullan told me she was okay and easy to get, if you once got to know her. And the May devotions are on the way. Long evenings. Warm grass. And Frank Mullan should know. He knows them all.

Of course it goes without saying that the devotions on May evenings in the parish church, with the high, limping, Gothic spires, went away back to something far before the worship of holy purity and the blessed virgin, to some pagan festival of the rites of spring. This he found out afterwards by reading, and by much dull talk, in more sophisticated places, heaven help us, than his own native town. But in the spring of that year he neither knew nor worried about such things, as he knelt beside Tom Cunningham in the side aisle to the left hand of the high altar.

Oh, those brown angels cut in wood of a slightly lighter colour than the wood of the beams to which they provided a figurehead finish. They swooped out towards each other over the nave and eyed the praying people. Once he had tried to write a poem about them:

> In church the angels cut in wood
> In row on row arranged
> Stand always as before they stood,
> And only I am changed.

But it wouldn't work. The angels weren't standing, for God's sake, they had no legs or feet to stand on, or, if they had, those legs were buried in the wood of the beams from which winged torsos and long-haired oaken heads seemed to have instantaneously, ecstatically, emerged.

Times, he still saw those angels in his dreams, soaring, in a sort of a way, over altar, incense, monstrance, praying priest, responding mumbling people, over Tom Cunningham in the side aisle making cute sideways eyes and secrets signs at Sadie Law who knelt with her favourite friend directly under the angels in the nave. Whatever about bullshit talk and the rites of spring, the devotions on May evenings was where you met people for good or evil; and all around the church, high on a hill with its hopalong spires, the rolling country was rich in deep grass and the birds were making mocking calls along hidden lovers' lanes. The high grassy embankments along the railways that went out of the town to the Donegal sea at Bundoran, or to Dublin or Belfast, or down then by Derry to the northern sea, were a sort of secret world where only lovers went in the long evenings. No respectable girl would be seen walking along the railway. The art was in not being seen.

His daughter, who was eighteen years of age, said to his mother who admitted to being eighty-five: Dad must have been happy here in this town in his schooldays. He's always singing a song. Well, not singing exactly. It has no particular tune. No beat. Dad's a bit of a square. It goes more like an African chant.

— Wallawalla boom boom, said his son who was fourteen.

— John, said the daughter, mind your manners. Granny doesn't dig Swahili. No granny. The song begins like this. Thrice happy and blessed were the days of my childhood and happy the hours I wandered from school, by green Mountjoy's forest, our dear native wildwood, and the green flowery banks of the serpentine Strule.

— Mountjoy forest, he said, was part of the estate of Lord and Lady Blessington. Back in the days of the great Napoleon. That was an old song.

— He was a good scholar, his mother said. He was very fond of reading poetry out loud. In the mornings after breakfast. Before he went to school.

As if he wasn't there at all. His daughter giggled.

He was accustomed to his mother rhapsodising in this way, talking about him to other people in his presence. Once she had said to a friend of his: He would be the best man in Ireland if it wasn't for the little weakness.

Afterwards his friend had said with great good humour: with you standing there I couldn't very well ask her which weakness she meant.

Another time and under similar circumstances she had said to the same friend: His father, God rest him, put on some weight when he passed forty, but he never swelled like that.

Pointing to him. As if, by God, the son, had had a dropsical condition.

To her grand-daughter and grandson she said: He read Shelley. If Winter comes can Spring be far behind. I liked that. Shelley was a good poet. Although my own mother could never understand about Tennyson and the brook. She used to say: Poor fellow, could nobody stop him. I think she thought it was about some unfortunate man that had something astray about his bowels. Then there was one poet that droned on and on about Adam and Eve and the fall of Satan.

She spat mildly and politely towards the fireplace where, winter or summer, there was always a fire. She preserved many old country customs. One was to spit when, by inadvertence or necessity, one mentioned a name of the devil – and his names were legion.

Twenty-eight years later he was still a little ashamed that he had inflicted on his mother's patient ears the monotony of Milton, even to the utter extremity of the Latin verses.

— Milton, he said, a bit of a bore.

But nobody paid the least attention to him. So he closed his eyes and his mind to the lot of them: the mother, old, wrinkled, wearing a battered old felt hat that looked like a German helmet, but with an eye as bright and inquisitive as it must have been when she was a lively singing country girl, and the man she was to marry was walking round and round the South African veldt; and he himself wasn't even a fragment of an imagination, or a gleam or a glint in his father's eye; the daughter, pert, small, lively, endlessly talkative; the son, tall, easy-going, slouching when he walked – as his grandfather had done. It was uncanny to observe such resemblances.

Since not one of the three of them paid any attention to him he shut his eyes and his mind to them and went on his own through the town, and back to the past that had made the town and him.

The two tall limping Gothic spires rose high above the hilly narrow streets. Those two spires and the simple plain spire for the Protestant church – that would be Church of Ireland for the Methodists and Presbyterians did not rise to spires – could be seen for a distance of ten miles. They soared, they were prayers of a sort, over the riverine countryside.

The taller spire was all of two hundred and thirty feet high, thirty of that being for the surmounting cross. To climb up the inside of that spire you went first by a winding stone stairway to the organ loft, then by a steep straight wooden stairway to the shaky creaky platform where the sexton stood when he pulled the bell-rope, then up a series of perpendicular ladders to the place where the two bells were hung, sullen and heavy, but ready at the twitch of a rope to do their duty. From that eminence, one hundred and fifty feet up, you could look down on everything. The town was almost flat, no longer all humps and hills and high ridged roofs and steep narrow streets. Down there was the meeting place of two rivers, the Camowen and the Drumragh: a sparkling trout-water, a sullen pike-water. Who could comprehend the differences there were between rivers, not to speak now of the Amazon and the Seine and the Volga and the Whang-ho and the Ohio, but even between neighbouring rivers destined to marry and to melt into one? United, the waters of Drumragh and Camowen went on under the name of the Strule, sweeping in a great horseshoe around the wide holm below the military barracks, tramping and tossing northwards to meet yet another river, the Fairywater, then to vanish glistening into a green-and-blue infinity.

Except you were the sexton, or some lesser person

authorised by him, you were not, by no means, supposed
to be up there at all. Dusty boards, with crazy, dizzy gaps
between them, swayed and bent under your feet. Vicious
jackdaws screeched. The blue-and-green infinity into
which the sparkling water vanished was the place where
Blessington's Rangers had once walked, speaking Gaelic,
great axes on shoulders. They cut down the trees to make
timber for war against Bonaparte, and money to keep
Lord and Lady Blessington, their daughter, and the inef-
fable Count D'Orsay gallivanting.

One day coming home from school alone – that was a
time of the day when it wasn't easy to be alone but, with
cunning, it could be managed – he had found the door
at the foot of the stone stairway open and had taken the
chance that it was open by accident. It was. He made the
climb. He saw the world. He was alone with the jackdaws
and the moan of the wind. Then on the way down the
perpendicular ladders he had missed a rung, slipped,
screamed with the jackdaws, grabbed desperately and
held on. Just about where the sexton would stand to pull
the bell-rope he had vomited a sort of striped vomit that
he had never seen before. Even in boyhood there was the
fear of death.

Nobody, thank God, had ever found out who had thus
paid tribute, made offertory, in the holy place. For weeks
afterwards he had felt dizzy even when climbing the stairs
to his bedroom.

When the war was over and Boney beaten, the gallivanting lords and ladies had no more use for the woodsmen
of Mountjoy. For the last time they walked down there

below in the old Flax Market that hadn't changed much since 1820: in their rough boots and frieze coats, axes on shoulders, speaking a guttural language that was doomed almost to die, singing, drinking, fighting among each other, but standing shoulder to shoulder or axe to axe against the world. The paltry townsmen and shopkeepers must have breathed easily when the woodsmen went north to Derry to board the American boat.

As a boy he had known of them and walked among their shadows in the Old Market: No more will we see the gay silver trout playing, or the herd of wild deer through its forest be straying, or the nymph and gay swain on its flowery bank straying, or hear the loud guns of the sportsmen of Strule.

On those may evenings the steeplejacks were swinging on the spires, tiny black dwarfs sitting in wooden chairs at the ends of ropes. They were pointing the stones, which meant that they smeared in fresh cement, netted the soaring prayers in nets of new white. Snug and secure in deep warm grass on a railway embankment from which there was a view both of the tips of the roofs of the town and of one deep curve of the slow pike-infested Drumragh River, Tom and Sadie, Tom's friend and Sadie's friend, lay on their backs and watched the dwarfs on the steeples.

— Why, Angela said, did they not build one steeple as long as the other?

— As high, he said, you mean.

— High or long, she said, what's the difference?

She had a wide humorous mouth that, some evening, with the help of God, he would get around to kissing.

— It all depends, Tom said, on which way you're going. Like up or down or sideways.

— Why, she repeated.

She was a stubborn girl. He held her hand.

— In this life, Tom said, there is nothing perfect.

— No, he said.

Because he knew.

— Two men were killed on the smaller steeple. So they stopped.

— Brian, said Tom, always has a better story. Say us a poem, Brian.

— That's no story. It's gospel truth.

Tom and Sadie were kissing, gurgling. Angela tickled his palm.

— That's a job, he said, I wouldn't have for all the tea in China.

He meant being a steeplejack.

Tom surfaced. He said: I'm not so sure. I wouldn't mind being able to get up as high as that.

Sadie said: You could always try.

With her left hand she gently massaged Tom's grey-flannelled crotch.

He watched Sadie's small moving hand. He wondered how many people within a ten-mile radius, in the town, in villages, from farmhouse doorways, walking along laneways, or fishing, or lying on grass, were watching the steeplejacks on the spires.

For no reason that he could explain he thought it would be exciting to see that face again, the wide humorous mouth, the brown hair that curled like two little brown horns over her temples, the plump fresh cheeks. The hair, though, wouldn't be brown any more. Don't forget that. Look for something older. Three years older than yourself: a reasonable gap of years, once upon a time, for a girl who could teach and a boy who was willing, even afraid, to learn.

— That woman, his daughter said, who writes you those letters from Indiana. What part of this town did she live in? When she was a girl, I mean.

The three of them were walking down the steep High Street. Behind and above them, where two narrower streets met to form the High Street, was the eighteenth-century courthouse, high steps before it and Doric columns, dominating the long, undulations of High Street and Campsie Avenue until the houses ended and the point of vision was buried in deep trees.

He told them that there had once been in the town a policeman so lazy that he hated to walk. So he sat all day, when the day was sunny, on the courthouse steps. When his superior officers asked him what he thought he was at, he defended himself by saying that he had the whole town under observation.

This grey day, the last sad day but one of the old year, would have been no day for sitting on the steps.

They laughed at the memory of the lazy policeman, and descended the steep street. The daughter said: You never met her, all the times you were in the States?

— I never even met her, I only saw her, when we were young together here in this town. She's a shadow, a memory.

— Shadows, she said precisely, don't write letters.
Memories might.

— One time last year, he said, I had hoped to meet her.
I was, so to speak, passing that way. That is, within a few
hundred miles or so of where she lives. That's not far, out
there.

— Just next door, his son said.

— It was in March, he said, and I was on the way north
to give a lecture in Minnesota. I crossed Indiana.

— See any Injuns dad, said the son.

— No, what I mostly remember about Indiana is big
barns and ducks, the big ducks that we call Muscovy
ducks, anywhere else in the world.

— But then dad, his daughter said, you never were in
Muscovy.

— Or if he was, said the son, he never told us.

In March in Indiana the endless flat brown land still
shivered. The harness-racing tracks by the roadside were
soggy and empty. The last of the snow lay here and there
in sordid mounds. Cattle, with a certain guilty look about
the, foraged among the tall battered corn-stalks of last
year's harvest. There was ice at the fringes of creeks and
rivers that looked far too small to negotiate such interminable expanses of flat land. Great round-roofed barns
stood aloof from, yet still dwarfed, the neat houses. Flat
and sombre the land went every way to a far horizon . . .

— A small American penny, his daughter said, for your
wandering thoughts.

He told her that in one small field near the city of
Lafayette he had seen a flock of more than two hundred

Muscovy ducks. The field had been between a railway and a line of power pylons.

— Nothing, he explained, more emphasises distance in flat land than a line of pylons striding on and on for ever, giants marching, carrying cables on their shoulders, until they vanish east or west.

— Or north or south, his son said.

— Now, she said sweetly, we know all about electricity. Dad, you're such a dear old bore. We couldn't care less about ducks or pylons. We want to know about the woman who writes you those marvellous letters from Indiana.

— She was an orphan, he said. In an orphanage. In Derry City.

— So far so good, his son said.

— She was taken out of the orphanage by this woman and reared in this town. She suffered a lot from illness. She wore a leg-splint when she was a child. She grew up. She read books. My father used to talk a lot about her. He used to say: You should meet that young woman. She's a wonder.

— But I was in college in Dublin, by that time, coming and going and somehow or other I never did get the opportunity of speaking to her. My memory is of a rather long beautiful face, sort of Madonna, and fair hair. Framed like an old picture in glass and wood, against a background of coloured magazines and paperbacked books. Because my last recollection of her is that she was working in the bookstall in the railway station. During the war she went off to London, married an American. Then seven or eight years ago she read something I'd written and wrote to me. That's the whole story.

She had written: You may have a vague recollection of who I am when you read my name. Then again you may not. It's been a long time. About thirty years. But I remember you very well, indeed: on your way to school, to church, walking the roads around our time, always, it seemed to me, alone.

That would be a romantic young girl confusing an average sullen lout of a fellow with her private image of Lord Byron.

— We rarely said more than hello. We lived in the same town all our growing years. We walked the same roads, knew the same people, and didn't meet at all. We might have shared a common interest. I loved books, poetry, music, but had little opportunity to enjoy any of them. I did manage to read quite a lot, and to remember poetry, and get a little music on an old radio. I walked, and thought of the books I'd read, and repeated the poetry to myself, and could hear the music again along the quiet roads. Thus I survived the town I was born in. Though mostly I remember it with love, because of Margaret, the woman who reared me. She was gentle, poor, uneducated, but with a lively mind and kind to all things livihg – especially to me when she took me from the nightmare of the orphanage in Derry, haunting me even now with its coldness, the crooked hilly streets of Derry, the jail, the Diamond, the wide Foyle which is really our own Strule, and the ships.

— Another penny for your thoughts, his daughter said. Or a measly nickel.

They turned right from the Market Street along the

Dublin Road, past a filling station and a Presbyterian church, a toy-like gasworks, the old white houses of Irishtown. Beyond Irishtown, he told them, was the Drumragh River and the old humped King's Bridge where James Stuart, falling back from the walls of Derry, had watched the town burn behind him.

Then they were ascending through a pleasant affluent suburb.

— No, he said, this wasn't the part of the town she lived in. We're not going that way just at the moment.

They were, in fact, walking to say a prayer at his father's grave. Everywhere he went he carried with him for luck a white stone from the grave. A white stone from the grave of a kind man would have to be lucky, wouldn't it, if there was the least pick of reason in the universe? But in a drunken moment in Dublin City he had loaned the stone to a man who ran greyhounds, and this particular greyhound had won, and the man begged to be allowed to keep the stone. Today he would say his prayer and take away with him another white stone.

The Protestants lay to the left of the cemetery's main avenue, the Catholics to the right, and between them, on a slight rise, the stone oratory, cold and draughty, where on harsh days the last prayers were said over the coffins. He never remembered the wind around the corners of that oratory as being, even in summer, anything but bitterly cold. This last dead day, but one, of the year it was unbearable. Bravely the boy and girl knelt on the damp earth and prayed. He knelt with them, not praying, talking without words to the man under the clay, or somewhere in the air around him, and around him wherever in the world he went: the dead hover for ever over the living.

Low dark clouds travelling, or being forced to travel, fast, bulged with rain. To the lee of the empty oratory the three of them stood and looked over the forest of obelisks and Celtic crosses, sacred Hearts and sorrowing mothers, at the distant sweep of the flooded Drumragh, at where the railway line used to cross it by a red metal bridge. The bridge was gone and the railway too – sold for scrap. But three hundred yards to the east of the river, there was still the stone bridge under the embankment – it looked like a gateway into an old walled city – and the lovers' lane that led into the fields, and across the fields to the wooded brambly slope above one of the deepest, most brooding of the river's pike-pools.

Would it be sin or the beginning of living to touch the hidden flesh of Angela? His dream of fair women was all about the creeping hand, the hair, the warmth. That was all that Tom and the other boys talked about.

She lay on her back in the brambly wood – the pike hovering in the pool below them – and he fumbled fearfully, and tickled her, his hand timidly outside her dress. But when she reached for him he rolled away. She laughed for a longer time than seemed necessary. From the far side of a clump of bushes he heard Tom say to Sadie: There must be nothing in Brown's house that doesn't smell of embrocation.

— The grave was very weedy, the daughter said.

— So I noticed. Your grandmother pays good money to

have it kept clean and covered with white stones. On the way out I'll call to the caretaker's house and talk to him.

The clay in the centre of the grave had sunk. He was glad that neither son nor daughter had noticed that. It would be so painful to have to explain to the young people, or even to oneself, that clay sank so when the coffin underneath had collapsed.

The hotel they stopped in was a mile outside the town, a domed mid-nineteenth-century house, miscalled a castle, on a hill top with a view of the heathery uplands the Camowen came from, and quite close to a park called the Lovers' Retreat, but known to the soldiers in the barracks as Buggers' Den.

The aged mother was safely at home in bed, in her small house across the narrow street from those gigantic limping spires. She liked to be close to the quietness of the church, the glowing red circle around the sanctuary lamp where she remembered and prayed for and to the dead man.

Leaving her in peace they had walked through the lighted crowded town, along a quiet dim suburban road, over a bridge that crossed the invisible talkative Camowen – there was a good gravelly trout pool just below that bridge. They dined late in a deserted dining-room. Along a corridor there was the noise of merriment from the bar. His son asked him which room had been the haunted room in the days when the hotel had been a castle.

— For the sake of the ghost, the daughter said, let's hope it wasn't where the bar is now.

— Ghosts, he told her, might like company.

— Not mine I pray, she said.

— Fraidy cat, the son said. A ghost couldn't hurt you.

— That ghost, he told them, couldn't hurt anyone. The story was that the people who lived her called in the priest and he blessed the room and put the ghost in a bottle.

— Poor ghost, she said.

— But where, she wondered, did the priest put the bottle.

— On the river, the son said. And it floated over the sea to England, and somebody found it and opened it, and got a ghost instead of a message.

He saw them to their rooms. No ghost could survive in such up-to-date comfort. No ghost could rest in peace in any of the coloured bottles in the bar. The noisy local drinkers had gone home, taking their din with them. A few commercial men, talking of odds and ends, drinking slowly but with style, sat in an alcove. He joined them.

— Did you like it out there, they asked him.

— You were a friend of Tom Cunningham, they said.

— It's good out there. Fine people. Hospitable. The sort of people I meet.

— Tom went into the Palestine police after the war, they said. Then he went farther east. Never heard of since.

— Chasing the women in China, they said.

— But the crime in America, they said. Did you ever come up against that?

— It's there. But I never came up against it. Except in the newspapers.

— By God, they said, they have picturesque murders out there. We never have anything here except an odd friendly class of a murder. But out there. That fellow in Chicago and the nurses. And the young fellow that made the women in the beauty parlour lie down like the spokes of a wheel and then shot the living daylights out of them.

— The one that sticks most in mind . . .

They were all attention.

. . . was the girl in the sump. This sump is an overflow pond at the back of a dry-cleaning plant. One morning a man walking by sees a girl's leg standing up out of the water.

— Clothed in white samite, they said. Mystic, wonderful.

— Seems she had been by day a teller in a bank and by night a go-go dancer in a discotheque. One day she walks out of the bank with a bagful of thousands of dollars. She is next encountered in the sump, one leg surfacing, her hands tied behind her back, her throat cut, the bag and the dollars gone. A barman from the discotheque is also missing.

— All for love, they said.

The long cold day, the search for the past, the drink, the warm company, had made him maudlin.

— When I read the newspapers today there are times I think I was reared in the Garden of Eden.

— Weren't we all, they said.

But it hadn't been the Garden of Eden for one waif of a girl, now a woman in far-away Indiana. From Atlanta, Georgia, where he had been for two years he had remailed to her the local newspapers that had come to him from this town.

She had written: That photograph of the demolition of the old stone railway bridge at Brook Corner saddened me. I recall that bridge with affection. When I'd spent about fourteen months flat on my back in the County Hospital, and was at last permitted up on crutches, I headed, somewhat shakily, under that bridge to begin the first of many walks. I still remember the bridge framing the road beyond like a picture, and the incredible green of the fields, the flowering hedges, the smell of hawthorn. The bridge became for me a gateway: to happy solitude. When I had trachoma and thought I might go blind my bitterest thought was that I might never again see the world through that bridge. Margaret's brother, Fred, was my companion and consolation in those dark days. He had been hired out at the age of six to work with a farmer and Margaret remembered seeing the golden-curly-haired child going off in the farmer's trap.

— Perhaps that was why Fred never cared to work. He hadn't, for about twenty-five years before he died, not he couldn't but simply because he didn't want to. Oh, on a number of occasions, he worked, briefly, for farmers at harvest time, was rarely paid in cash but in kind; and only on condition that his dog, Major, could accompany him. Major barked all day, every day, as though indignant at his master's labours, and much to the chagrin of the other workers and the farmer. But since, when he wanted to, Fred could work as well as the others, his services were always desired and he was permitted to stay, dog and all.

— He was a strange silent man who sat by the fire all day with a far-off look in his eyes. He had very blue eyes.

He rarely spoke to anyone outside the house. He was my sole companion during many long hours when I was confined to bed. I would read to him and ask him to spell and he would deliberately mis-spell and would be delighted when I would sharply correct him. I never knew how much I loved him until he died.

— Margaret housekept for Morris, the lawyer, who lived in the Georgian house beside the church with the high spires, and that left Fred and me a lot alone, and Fred would cook for me. Once, after I had been with Margaret several months, some sadistic neighbour woman told me that I was being sent back to the orphanage. So terrified was I that I hobbled up to the church and stood for hours across the street from the lawyer's house, waiting, the wind moaning away up in the spires in the darkness, until Margaret came and comforted me, led me home by the hand to Fred and Major and numerous cats, and a one-legged hen who had a nest in the corner and who was infuriated if another hen ever came to the back door in search of scraps.

His room was haunted, sure enough. He had sat too late, drunk too much, perhaps released the ghosts from the bottles. Oaken angels sang from the ceiling. A tearful crippled girl waited in the darkness at the foot of spires lost also in the windy darkness, no longer magic towers from which one could see the world. The leg of a girl who had stolen for love stood up like a stump of wood out of stagnant water.

Very cautiously he had asked his mother: Do you

remember a family called Law? Are they still in the town? One of them, I think, was a famous racing cyclist.

Cautiously: because in her eyes there were times when he was still fourteen or less and there were people that he wasn't supposed to know.

— Oh, I remember the Laws. They were famous, indeed.

Around the house she had a fancy for dressing as if she were a pirate chief. Or perhaps it was a gipsy queen. Sometimes instead of the helmet-shaped hat she wore a white gipsy head-handkerchief; and a long red dressing-gown and a Galway shawl with the corners tucked back under her oxters and pinned behind.

— One of them called in to see me one morning after Sunday mass. A Law or a half Law or a quarter-Law or a by-Law. You wouldn't have much time for the like of them. Not condemning anyone for the weakness, but there were more distant cousins in that clan than was natural. Or godly.

That seemed to be that.

— You wouldn't have expected much of the Laws, she said. But it's heartrending to see the fate of some families that had every chance that God and man could give them.

— Like who, for instance?

— Like many I've seen. Like the Glenshrule family, for one.

The red bull of Glenshrule roared through his haunted dreams.

— Glenshrule's sold, she said, and in the hands of strangers.

The bull, he supposed, had been sold to make Bovril.

Two private roadways led into the old house at Glenshrule, one from the steep by-road along which the crippled girl had hobbled to find peace, one from the road that led west to the Donegal sea. To either hand on either road it was all Glenshrule land, green, bountiful, a little unkempt, cattle country, little tillage. The three bachelor brothers of Glenshrule were gentlemen farmers: which meant whipcord breeches and booze and hunting horses. But they were frank, reckless, generous, easy in their money and good breeding, and made no objection to the townspeople using their private roads for circular walks on Sunday afternoons. Roving boys used those roads all the time, and the fields around them, and the only prohibiting notice to be seen told you to beware of the red bull.

— Christ, look at the size of him, Tom cried with an artist's enthusiasm. Boy, if you were built like that you'd be welcome anywhere.

They sat on a five-barred iron gate. Between them and the bull's private meadow was the additional fortification of a strong wooden gate. He was an unruly bull. His red coat shone. He had a head near as big as the head of the mouldy bison they had seen in the Old Market in Bostock and Wombell's travelling menagerie. He rooted at the ground with one fore-foot. The great head rose and fell. He didn't roar. He rumbled all the time like a train, far away, going into a tunnel.

— There's a lot to be said, Tom said, for being a bull.

— Everybody puts up with your tantrums.

— There's more to it than that.

— Then the lady of Glenshrule, the one single sister of the three bachelor brothers, rode by on a bay mare. To acknowledge that they existed she raised her riding-crop, she smiled and said: Don't tempt him. Don't enter the meadow. Bulls eat boys.

— Boys, Tom muttered.

He was very bitter.

There's also a lot to be said, he said, for being a bay mare.

She was bareheaded. She was blonde. She was twenty-five. She was blonde, she was blonde, she was blonde and calm-faced, and all the officers in the barracks pursued her. Years afterwards – altering the truth, as memory always does – he thought that he had then thought about queen and huntress, chaste and fair. But he hadn't. He had been too breathless to think of anything except, perhaps, that Sadie and Angela, lively and provoking as they could be, were still only in the servant-maid class.

She rode on towards the Donegal road. The sound of the hooves died away. The red bull, calmed, had lain down on the grass.

— One Sunday evening I sat beside her in the church, Tom said. My right leg against her left. It burned me. I can feel it still.

He rubbed his right thigh slowly, then sniffed his hand.

— I swear to God, he said, she pressed her thigh against mine. It made short work of the holy hour.

That was the year Tom and himself had been barred from the town's one cinema because Tom, ever an eager and

enquiring mind, had discovered the anti-social use of hydro-
gen sulphide. A few sizzling test-tubes planted here and
there in the darkness could have tumultuous effects on the
audience. Old Mr. Pritchard – he was so old that it was suspected he had fought in the Zulu war – was heard to say in
a barrack-square voice that some bloke here needed a purge
of broken bottles. But three burly ushers simply purged Tom
and his companion from the audience, two of them to hold
Tom, the other to herd the companion before him.

Such a splendid deed and its consequences gave the
two of them the glory of outlaws among their contem-
poraries. And to be barred from the delights of Eddy
Cantor's Rome, or of Broadway with its gold-diggers, or
of Wallace Beery's Big House, meant more nights in the
Old Flax Market. That was fair enough, because the Old
Flax Market was the place for outlaws. Black-uniformed
constables patrolled the streets but, unless there was very
audible drunken disorder, they left the Old Flax Market
alone. No flax was ever sold there any more.

— The ghosts of the woodsmen are still here, he told
Tom. This was their place when they came to town.

— You and those bloody woodsmen. You're a haunted
man.

The unpaved three acres of the Old Market were
sodden and puddled. A sharply-defined half-moon cut
like a cleaver through wispy running clouds. He shouted at
the moon: No more will the fair one of each shady bower
hail her dear boy of that once happy hour, or present him
again with a garland of flowers that they oft times selected
and wove by the Strule.

— And poetry, boy, will be your ruination. Poetry will get you nowhere with Angela. Move in man. Angela demands action.

The moon, even if it was only half a moon, was useful to outlaws in a land of outlaws. For there were only three gas-lamps in the whole of the Old Flax Market and gas-lamps were little use on windy nights or when somebody, for fun or helleri, wished to quench them. One lamp was on a wall-bracket at the corner of a rowdy dance hall. It lighted, when it was allowed to, the wooden stairway to the door of the dance hall, and the people ascending or descending or standing in groups making noise. One lamp lighted the covered cobbled entry-way from the High Street. The third lighted the muddy uncovered exit to a dark riverside walk from which an irate lover had, about that time, heaved his fancy into the river.

— Let's have a look, Tom said, at the Jennet's corner. You'd see things there you never saw at the pictures.

— But look, he said, there goes the Bluebottle, her legs like elevenpence marked on a new bucket.

The drum boomed, the horn blared from the dance hall. The half-moon coldly shone on the Strule waters that flowed by one side of the Old Market.

— If your woodsmen ever walked here you can bloody well guess what they were after.

A tall thin girl in a blue coat was being eased into the shadows by a drunken man.

— Would you believe it, Tom said, she fought like a cat here one night with one of the Fighting McDermotts.

The one with the dinge in his temple where some decent man brained him with a bottle of port-wine. When she wouldn't go with him he shouted he'd tell her father that sent her out for money, and her uncle that broke her in. She tore the red face off him.

— He rings the bell, her uncle.

— They say he rang the bell for her when she was thirteen.

There then was the terror of the dark walk by the river. The uncle who rang the bell as one of the last town-criers was a figure out of a German fairy-tale, a pied piper, tall hard hat, tailed coat, long grey moustache, a small man with a voice of thunder, swinging his handbell, shouting out fragments of news: that a group of strolling players would perform in the town hall, that the water supply would be turned off – for repairs to pipes in this or that part of the town, that such and such a house property would be auctioned. Was it credible that a comic fairy-tale figure should also be part of some sniggering story? The Bluebottle vanished ahead of them into some riverside bushes. Where the river made an elbow bend a group of smoking muttering men waited at the Jennet's corner. Her shady bower was a wooden shelter put there by the town council to protect Sunday walkers from sudden showers. The council had not intended to cater for the comfort of the Jennet and her customers. She was a raw-boned red headed country girl whose husband was in the mental hospital.

— Good natured and charges very little, Tom said.

Some of the shadowy courtiers called after them.

— But, boy, a little bit too open to the general public for men of taste like ourselves. Take me back to sweet sinful Sadie. Or the lady of Glenshrule on her bay mare.

She rode on the Donegal road, the hooves dancing clippety-clop, and the bull lay down in the meadow.

— What went wrong there, he said to his mother. They had everything.

— What would go wrong but debt and drink and the want of wit. The three brothers fled to Canada.

— They followed the woodsmen.

His mother didn't hear him.

— And my, she said, she looked lovely when she rode out astraddle on that bay mare.

— Tom Cunningham would have agreed with you.

— Oh, Tom Cunningham was a rare one. Very freckled when he was a little boy. And curly-haired. I'm amazed you remember him. He went to the war and never came back when it was over. But then you always had a good memory.

— I always had.

— She lived alone after the brothers left, and she never married, and went on drinking. There was a bit of scandal, too. But I never paid much attention to that sort of talk. She died in the ambulance on the way to hospital. But not, thank God, without the priest. For one of the curates was driving past just at that moment.

On the road she had ridden over on the bay mare.

— The Lord, his mother said, has everything mixed with mercy.

— He must have a lot of mercy for orphans, he said.

— Tell granny that story, dad, about the girl in the rain. The woman who writes to you. When she was a child, I mean.

She could still be outside there, the ghost of a frightened child, standing in the darkness at the foot of the spires. But one day in the orphanage playground she had broken out in rebellion.

— A sudden storm came up. The nuns called us in. we were to shelter, cold and miserable, in a sort of arcade or cloister. I started in with the rest, but suddenly I stopped and ran back to the playground. It was pouring. I was alone. The nuns called me. I wouldn't come. I danced around that playground in my bare feet, hair and dress soaking wet. Repeated calls failed to move me. Two nuns came after me. I ran and danced from one side to the other, dodging the hands that tried to clutch me. I laughed and danced in the wind and rain. I'd wait until they got close and then I'd run like the wind. Their long robes were heavy with water. They were exhausted. But I was exhilarated. Until suddenly I collapsed and was dragged inside. Mute and terrified and expecting to be lashed. I don't know why, but my defiance was forgiven.

— It was a ballet, his daughter said. The truant in the rain.

— Nuns on the run, said the son.

The German poet, long ago, went walking in the botanical gardens, saw plants, that elsewhere he had seen only in pots or under glass, growing cheerfully under the open sky. Might he not discover among them, the original plant from which all others are derived? After all, the poet thought, it must exist, the innermost nucleus.

A crazy idea. A wise old woman dressed like a gipsy or a pirate chief. A pert young girl curious about the American woman who had once been an orphan child in this town. Sadie Law with her leather coat and the smell of embrocation. A blonde horse-riding queen and huntress dying of drink in the back of an ambulance. Two sad creatures, nicknamed, one for the colour of her only coat and the hard meagre shape of her body, the other because it was said, with sniggers, that she was hopeless of progeny and disreputable in her ancestry. Angela running hand in hand with him on a wet Saturday afternoon through the Old Flax Market.

The place was empty that day. Not even the ghosts of the woodsmen walked in the grey light and the rain. He couldn't remember where Sadie and Tom had been at the time. The Jennet's corner was also empty. In the wooden shelter, hacked with names and odd obscenities and coy references to local love affairs, they sat on a creaky seat and kissed and fumbled. Then around a corner of the shelter came the Jennet herself, leading a staggering cattle-drover, his ash-plant in his hand.

— Wee fellow, he said with great camaraderie, I suppose you're at the same game as myself.

— He's too bashful, Angela said.

— He'll live to learn, the Jennet said. They all do.

The rain ran down her bony face. Wet yellow hair stuck out from under a red tam o'shanter. Her eyes were of such a bright blue as to make her seem blind.

— The good book, the drover said, says that the wise man falls seven times. And, as sure as my name is Solomon, I'm going to fall now.

So the wee fellow retreated from the shelter, dragging Angela with him for a little way until she dug her heels into the muddy ground. The river was a brown fresh, taking with it broken branches and hay from flooded meadows, sweeping on, down then by Derry our dear boys are sailing. Now he remembered that that day Angela had been wearing a sou'wester and Sadie's black coat, a little big for her but a stronghold against the rain.

— What do we need to run for? You might learn something.

He said nothing.

— Wee boy, she said. I'm going back for a peep.

He stood alone looking at the turbulent river, looking across the river at the limping spires, one proud and complete, one for ever unfinished, a memory of defeat and death. What would a wild woodsman have done? Down along the river valley it was said that there were trees on which the woodsmen, just before they left had carved their names so strongly that the letters could still be read. But that must be a fable, a memory out of the old song: Their names on the trees of the rising plantation, their memories we'll cherish, and affection ne'er cool. For where are the heroes of high or low station that could be compared with the brave boys of Strule?

— That was as good as a circus, Angela said. You've no idea in the world what you missed.

*

At breakfast in the hotel in the morning the chatty little waitress shook his belief in himself by saying to him and his children that she had never heard of anybody of his name coming from this town.

— The great unknown, his daughter said.

— Fooling us all the time, the son said. He came from Atlanta, Georgia.

But then it turned out that the waitress came from a smaller town twenty miles away and was only eighteen years of age.

— Off we go now, said the daughter, to see where granny came from.

— Bring no whiskey to Claramore, his mother said. There was always too much whiskey in Claramore. Returned Americans coming and going.

The son and daughter wished her a happy new year.

— Drive down the town first, she said. I owe a bill I must pay.

— Won't it wait?

She was dressed in high style: widow's black coat, high hat and veil, high buttoned boots for walking in country places.

— Never begin the new year in debt was a good maxim. I'll stick to it while I have breath.

Her grand-daughter, sitting beside her in the back of the hired car, giggled. Sourly he accepted the comments, one unconscious, one conscious, of two other generations on his own finances.

He drove down High Street. They waited for her outside a hardware shop. The sky was pale blue, cloudless, and last night's unexpected white frost lay on the roofs and spotted the pavements. His daughter said: Granny never heard of a credit card.

More sordidly the son said: Nor hire purchase. Nor a post-dated cheque.

— It was a different world, mes enfants. They paid their way or went without.

But he knew that he had never worked out where – in the world that he had grown into – that terrifying old-fashioned honesty had gone: no debt, no theft, no waste. Beggars were accepted, because Joseph and Mary and Child Jesus had gone homeless into Egypt. But debt was a sort of sin.

— Eat black bread first, she would say. But let no man say you're in his debt.

He had never taken to black bread. He hadn't told her that in a briefcase in the boot he had two bottles of Jack Daniels as a gift for his cousin – and for himself. A decent man could not with empty hands enter a decent house, and two bottles of American whiskey would be a fit offering to a house that had sent so many sons and daughters to the States.

She was back in the car again, settling her self like a Duchess, her small red-headed grand-daughter helping her to tuck a rug around her knees. She refused to believe that a moving vehicle could be heated like a house.

It was a twelve-mile drive, first down the Derry road, over the steep hill that, in spite of all the miracles of mac-adam, was called, as it had been called in the eighteenth century, Clabber Brae. Then west, over the Drumquin railway crossing. There was no longer any railway to cross. Once upon a time the crossing-keeper's daughter had been as famous as Sadie Law. Then by Gillygooley crossroads where, one June day, Tom and himself, coming tired from fishing perch in the Fairywater, had seen Angela climbing a gate into a ripe meadow just opened for the mower. Her companion was a stocky-shouldered blackavised soldier. That much they could see. A hundred yards ahead, Tom rested from his cycling and was silent for a long time. Then he said: Boy, I'd leave that one alone for the future.

— She's leaving me alone. Who's she with?

— The worst in the barracks. Fusilier Nixon. And he'll never rank higher.

— Why so?

— Four years ago when he came back from India he was all but drummed out for raping a slavey in the soldiers' holm.

— There's a great view of the holm from the tall spire.

— If you had been up there you could have seen the fun. His bacon was saved by a major whose life he saved, or something, in India. And God help the slaveys. The offspring of that bit of love at first sight is now toddling around Fountain Lane. I'll point him out to you some day. You'd have something in common.

They cycled on.

— I'll tell Sadie, Tom said, what we saw. Sadie has some sense. She wouldn't want to be seen in the company of Fusilier Nixon.

Their bicycles bumped over the railway crossing.

The keeper's daughter waved, and called: Hello, Tom Cunningham.

— Cheer up, boy. You'll get another girl.

— I suppose I will.

— From here to China the world's full of them.

— I liked Angela.

He found it hard not to sob. Angela peeping around a corner at the animals in the circus. Angela in the clutches of a black-chinned brute. He had, too, really liked her. More than thirty years later he foolishly looked for her face on the streets of the old town and the face he looked for could not, in reason, ever be there. He would see, instead, a Madonna – whom, also, he had never known – against a background of the coloured covers of magazines.

Now as he drove on, he looked at the gate Angela had climbed into the meadow. But one gate was very like another and, under white frost, all meadows were the same. Although this valley to him would always be summer holiday country. Every mile of it he had walked or cycled. A hay-shed by a prosperous farmhouse meant for him mostly the sultry July hush before the rain came, the smell of sheds and barns, heavy rain on tin roofs, or soda bread and strong tea by peat fires on open hospitable hearths.

There now across the stilled, white fields was the glint of water at the pool where Tom and himself would first strike the Fairywater. The road climbed here, up over the stony place of Clohogue, then switchbacked for miles in and out of hazel glens, over loud rough brooks, then on to a plateau, high, very high; and visible in such clear frosty air, and a good seventy miles away by the edge of the Atlantic, the pigback of Muckish Mountain, the white cone of Mount Errigal, the Cock of the North. Claramore was just below the plateau. It was a place of its own, in a new valley.

From the Barley Hill beyond the old long white farm-house you could also see those two far-away mountains and, in the other direction and looking down the valley of the Fairywater, the tips and crosses of the two limp-ing Gothic spires, but not the smaller plain spire of the Protestant church.

— On a calm evening, his cousin said, they seem so close that you'd imagine you could hear the bell ringing for the May devotions.

He asked his cousin: Do the young people still climb Drumard in autumn to pluck the blayberries?

— We've heard a lot about those same blayberries, his daughter said. To pluck and eat them, dad says, was a memory of some ancient pagan feast.

— The young people, his cousin said, have their own pagan feasts.

The four of them walked on the boreen that crossed the Barley Hill to the place where the men were build-ing a house for his cousin's son and the bride he would bring home with him in three months' time. Hard frost had slowed up the building work. Among the men, half-loitering, working just enough to keep warm, keeping as close as possible to an open brazier, his cousin passed round one of the bottles of bourbon. They drank from cracked cups and tin mugs, toasted the health of the visi-tors, of the bride-to-be, wished luck for ever on the house they were building. High above a jet plane, westward-bound out of Prestwick, made its mark on the cold pale blue.

— They'll be in New York before you, his son said.

The drinking men, circling the brazier, saluted the travellers in the sky and raised a cheer. It was only a few hours to New York from the Barley Hill or the pagan blayberries of Drumard. Breath ascended in puffs as white as the jet's signature. On the far side of the hill from the long farmhouse the Fairywater, glittering black, looped through frosted bottom-land.

— Phil Loughran, that used to work for you, he said. He was about my age. Where did he go?

The Black Stepping Stones were at that bend of the Fairywater, the seventh bend visible from where they stood; and above the Black Stones the pool where the country boys went swimming. Willows drooped over it. The bottom was good yellow sand. The water had the brown of the peat and was nowhere more than four feet deep. It was an idyllic place, had been an idyllic place until the day he had that crazy fight with Phil Loughran.

— He went to Australia, his cousin said. We hear he's doing well. The family, what's left of them, are still living here on my land.

Even to this day, and in the frosty air, he blushed to think of the lies he had told to Phil Loughran down there by the Black Stones – blushed all the more because, country boys being so much more cunning than towny boys, Phil almost certainly hadn't believed a word he said. Phil as he listened would have secretly laughed.

— So her name is Angela, he said.

Phil was a squat sallow-faced young fellow, dressed in rough corduroys and heavy nailed boots, his brown hair short-cropped, his eyes dark brown and close together. There was always a vague smell of peat smoke, or stables or something, from those corduroys.

— Angela the walking angel, he said.

They were dressing after a swim. Three other boys splashed and shouted in the pool. A fourth hung naked from a trailing willow, swinging like a pendulum, striking the water with his feet.

— So you tell us, Phil, you had the little man out of sight.

Then the two of them were rolling on the grass, swiping at each other, Phil still laughing, he sobbing, with temper, with the humiliation of having his tall tales of conquest made mockery of. Four naked dripping boys danced and laughed and shouted around them. It was the last day but one that he had been at the Black Stones. He had come second best out of that fight but he had a mean miserable sort of vengeance on his very last visit to the place.

Phil in his best corduroys – since it was Sunday – is crossing the water, stepping carefully from stone to stone, in his right hand the halter with which he is leading a love-stricken Claramore cow to keep her date with a bull on the farm on the far side of the river. So he calls to Phil to mind his Sunday-go-to-meeting suit and Phil, turning round to answer, is off his guard when the restive beast bolts. It is, fair enough, his turn to laugh, sharp, clear and cruel, as Phil, bravely holding on to the halter is dragged through the shallow muddy water below the stones. There are seventeen in Phil's family, and he is the eldest, and those corduroys will not be easily replaced.

Over the hard frosted fields his own laughter came back to him.

— I'm glad to hear he did well in Australia.

— They were a thrifty family, his cousin said. A sister of his might visit us this evening, the youngest of the breed, a god-daughter of mine.

The trail of the jet was curdling in the cold sky. The men had gone back to work. For penance he had told his cousin and son and daughter how he had laughed on the day the cow had dragged Phil through the muddy water. They stood by a huge sycamore a little down the slopes from the unfinished house. Icicles hung from bare branches. He said, nothing about how James had mocked his boasting.

— Weren't you the beast, dad, his daughter said.

— But it was funny, the son said.

— The young, his cousin said, can be thoughtless. Present company excepted.

For the daughter, the face of a good mimic distorted with mock fury, was dancing towards the cousin to stab him with an icicle broken from the sycamore.

— No, but seriously, he said when they had played out their pantomime of fury and terror: a grey man over sixty with a restful singing sort of voice and a pert little girl of sixteen.

— Seriously. Look at the sycamore. It was planted here more than a hundred years ago by an uncle of mine who was a priest. He died young, not long after ordination. He planted this tree on the day he was ordained, and blessed the earth and the sapling. You may recall, when you were young yourselves, some of his books were still about the house. Mostly Latin. Theology. Some novels. I told you about one of them and you rushed to get it. The *Lass of the Barns*, you thought I said. But, man alive, were you down in the mouth when you discovered it was the *Last of the Barons*.

— Oh dad, his daughter said.

— But I know the age of this tree by checking on the date on the priest's tombstone in Langfield churchyard. And my son says to me: We'll cut it down. It'll spoil the view from the new house. So I said: The house may fall, but this tree will stand while I do. The old have a feeling for each other.

— Lucky tree, the daughter said, that has somebody to stand up for it.

They went, laughing, back down the Barley Hill towards the warmth of the great kitchen of the farmhouse. Under the pall of the white frost it seemed as if nothing here would ever change: not the sycamore, not his cousin, nor the ancient sleeping land. Nothing would change, no matter how many airliners swept westwards up there, leaving nothing behind them but a curdling dissolving mark on the sky. All the ships that had carried all those people westwards, even so many sons and daughters of this house, and the ocean was still unmarked and the land here as it had been. It was elsewhere in the world the changes happened.

— But this fatal ship to her cold bosom folds them.
Wherever she goes our fond hearts shall adore them. Our
prayers and good wishes will still be before them, that their
names be remembered and sung by the Strule.

The pond at the corner of the avenue was frozen over.
He had fallen into it once, climbing the fence above and
beyond it to chase a wandering bullock out of a field of
young oats. The fence-post he had been holding on to had
broken. The water, he had always imagined, had tasted
of duck-dirt. But then how in hell would one be expected
to know what duck-dirt tasted like? The fence-post, he
noticed, was now made of iron, and that might be some
indication, even here, of change. But not much.

The ash-grove to the left before you came to the stables – in that grove he had once criminally broken a young
sapling to make a fishing rod – was now a solid wall of
grown strong trees, a windbreak on days of south-westerly
gales.

Would the horses in the stables be the same, with the
same names, as they had been thirty years ago? He was
afraid to ask, to be laughed at, to be told what he knew:
that even here, even loved familiar farmhouses didn't live
for ever. The dogs seemed to be the same – collies, with
more sprawling pups underfoot than had ever seemed
natural. The pattern of farming though, had changed
somewhat, he had been told: more barley, more pigs fed on
the barley, less oats, less root crops, more sucking calves
bred in season on the open pasture, taken early from their
mothers, and sold to be fattened somewhere in confine-
ment, and slaughtered.

In the house ahead of them somebody was playing a melodeon, softly, slowly, and that was something that hadn't changed, because in the past in that house there had been great country dances to pipe, fiddle and melodeon. That was before so many of his cousins, all much older than himself, had gone to the States.

His mother had enjoyed herself. She was red in the face and moist-eyed from sitting by the open hearth with its high golden pyramid of blazing peat; from remembering, for the instruction of younger generation, the comic figaries of her dear departed dowager of a sister, Kate, who, as a widow in her thirties, had ruled not only Claramore but half the countryside; and from, let it be admitted, sipping at the bourbon. For while she was a great one to lecture about the dangers of drink, she was liable the next minute to take from her sideboard a bottle of brandy and a bottle of whiskey, to ask what you were having, and to join you herself. And she instinctively thought the worst of a man who neither smoked, drank, swore, nor rode horses.

— The young people, she said, are growing up well, God bless them.

They haven't forgotten the old ways. That house was never without music and dancing.

The Claramore people had stood around the car, under a frosty moon, and sand Auld Lang Syne as their guests departed.

— That Loughran girl was a good hand at the melodeon. Did you all see her making up to the widow man, the returned American?

She poked him between the shoulder-blades as he drove slowly over the icy plateau.

— She sat on your knee, dad, the daughter said.

He could still feel the pressure of the underparts of the girl's thighs. She was conventionally slim and dark and handsome, with wide brown eyes; in appearance most unlike her eldest brother. She had sat on his knee in the dancing kitchen to tell him that Phil, in every letter he wrote from Australia, enquired about him. She stayed sitting there while his cousin sang: There was once a maid in a lonely garden when a well-dressed gentleman came passing by.

— Was that story true granny, the son asked. The one about the lone bush.

— Would I tell you if it wasn't.

They descended into the first hazel glen. Over the rushing of its brook they could hear the roaring of another jet, out of Prestwick, bound for New York.

— They're lining up to get into America, the son said.

— To get out of it too, son.

Six hours or so to the bedlam of Kennedy airport: But now our bold heroes are past all their dangers. On America's shores they won't be long strangers. They'll send back their love from famed Blessington's Rangers to comrades and friends and the fair maids of Strule.

People who left by jet left no shadows in old market-places. Generations would be born to whom the ache and the loneliness in the old songs of exile would mean nothing.

— Jordan Taggart the cobbler, as I said, had his house on the road from Claramore to Carrickaness, and a small farm to boot. Against the advice of all, even against Father

Gormley the priest that cured people, he cut down a whitethorn that grew alone in the middle of his meadow and, at nightfall, he dragged it home behind him for kindling. In the orchard before his house he saw two small children, dressed in white, and he spoke to them but they made no answer. So he told his wife and his three sons, who were also cobblers, that there were two shy children waiting, maybe for mended shoes in the orchard. But when two of the sons went out and searched they saw nothing. Then Jordan ate the supper of a healthy man and went to bed and died in his sleep.

— But he wasn't really dead, the son said.

— No, the white children took him. God between us and all harm.

In the darkness in the car she spat, but slightly and politely, and into the handkerchief.

The daughter said nothing.

They were back again in the meadow country where Angela had climbed the gate and, except for one last meeting, had climbed out of his life for ever. They bumped over the Drumquin crossing where there was no longer any railway to cross, no easy girl to call longingly after Tom Cunningham who was chasing girls in China and never wrote to enquire about anybody.

The daughter was alert again. She was giggling. She said: Dad, Granny wants to do something about the way you dress.

— I was only thinking about his own good, his mother said.

Although he was carefully driving the car over Clabber

Brae, he knew by the way she talked that he was no longer there.

— But when I was by the seaside at Bundoran I saw these young fellows wearing loose coloured patterned shirts outside their trousers. I was told it was an American fashion and I was sure that he would be wearing one of them when he came home.

He said: I'm no young fellow.

— What I thought was that it would cover his middle-aged spread.

As they descended by the military barracks into the town the daughter's giggles rocked the car.

— A maternity shirt, she said.

— For how could he expect anyone to look at him at his age and with a stomach like that.

Castle Street went up so steeply that it seemed as if it was trying to climb those dark grotesque spires.

— A young one, for instance, like that Loughran girl who sat on his knee because the chairs were scarce.

— That one, he said. All that I remember about the Loughrans is that her bare-footed elder brothers were always raiding Aunt Kate's cherry trees and blaming the depredation on the birds.

In the hotel bar only two of the commercial men were left. They said: What do you think now of your happy home town?

— How do you mean?

— Last night's tragic event, they said. Didn't you hear? Didn't you read the paper?

— I was in the country all day.

Back in the past where one didn't read the newspapers.

— A poor man murdered, they said. What your American friends would call a filling station attendant.

— Robbed and shot, they said. Just when we were sitting here talking about murder.

The grandfather clock in the hallway chimed midnight.

— The New Year, he said. May it be quiet and happy.

In the ballroom in the far wing of the hotel the revellers were clasping hands and singing about old acquaintance.

— We should be there singing, he said.

— The second murder here this year, they said. The other was a queer case, two young men, a bit odd. Things like that usen't to happen. This town is getting to be as bad as Chicago.

— It isn't as big or as varied.

They laughed. They agreed that the town was still only in a small way of business. He asked them was the park called Lovers' Retreat still where it had been.

— If that's the way you feel, it is.

More laughter.

— But it's gone to hell, they told him. It's not kept as it used to be. The young compulsory soldiers in national service wreck everything. They haven't the style of the old Indian army, when the empire was in its glory. Children's swings uprooted now. Benches broken. One of the two bridges over the millrace gone completely. The grass three feet long.

— Nothing improves, they said.

When they left him he sat on for a long time, drinking

alone. Was it imagination, or could he really hear the sound of the Camowen waters falling over the salmon leap at the Lovers' Retreat? That place was one of the sights of the town when the salmon was running: the shining curving bodies rising from the water as if sprung from catapults – leaping and struggling upwards in white foam and froth. But one year the water was abnormally low, the salmon a sullen black mass in the pool below the falls – a temptation to a man with Tom Cunningham's enterprise. The water-bailiff and his two assistants and his three dogs came by night and caught Tom and his faithful companion with torch and gaff and one slaughtered salmon. But since the bailiff, a bandy-legged amiable man, was also the park-keeper he said not a word to the police on condition that the two criminals kept the grass in the park mowed for a period of six months.

— Hard labour, by God, boy. He has us by the hasp. The Big House with Wallace Beery. You be Mickey Rooney.

The bad news travelled and was comic to all except the two mowers.

Then one day from the far side of the millrace that made one boundary to the park they heard the laughter of women, and saw Sadie and Angela, bending and pointing.

— Two men went to mow, they sang, went to mow the meadow.

— Grilled salmon for all, they called.

Tom crossed the millrace by leaping on to the trunk of a leaning tree that was rooted on the far bank. Sadie, laughing, screaming in mock terror, and Tom in pursuit, vanished into the bluebell woods. Tom's companion crossed the millrace prosaically by one of the wooden footbridges. Was it the one that the wild young resentful compulsory soldiers had destroyed? She didn't run. She wasn't laughing any more. Her brown hair no longer curled in little horns on her temples but was combed straight back. But the wide mouth, in spite of the black fusilier, was to him as inviting as ever. She said: You're a dab-hand at mowing. You've a future in cutting grass.

He said: I never see you any more.

— Little boys should take what's offered to them, when it's offered. Go back to your scythe.

— Go back to the fusilier, he said.

He went back to his scythe by climbing along the trunk of the leaning tree and leaping the millrace. The grass that fell before his scythe was crimson in colour and swathed in a sort of mist. The swing of the scythe moved with the rhythm of the falling water sweeping on to meet the Drumragh, to become the Strule, to absorb the Fairywater and the Derg and the Owenkillen, to become the Mourne, to absorb the Finn, to become the Foyle, to go down then by Derry to the ocean, taking with it the shadows of the woodsmen, the echoes of the brass and pipes and tramping feet of the army of a vanished empire, the stories of all who had ever lived in this valley.

He knew he was drunk when he heard the woman's voice speak respectfully to him and saw her through the crimson mist through which long ago he had seen the falling grass. She said: You wouldn't remember me, sir.

He didn't. She wore the black dress, white collar and

cuffs of the hotel staff. She would be sixtyish. She said: we saw you on the teevee one night and I said to Francie who you were. But he said he didn't know you. He knew your elder brother better.

— My brother was well known.

— Francie's my brother. You might remember he used to ride racing bicycles. I saw you in the dining-room. I work in the kitchen. I knew it was you when I saw your son, and from the teevee.

— You're Sadie Law.

— I didn't like to intrude on you and the children.

He said there was no intrusion. They shook hands. He asked her how her brother was.

— He's in a chair all the time. He broke his back at the tom-fool cycling. But he does woodcarving, and I work here. We manage. I never married.

Her face did not remind him of Sadie Law, but then he found that he could not remember what Sadie Law's face had looked like.

— Nobody, he said, could replace Tom Cunningham.

She neither smiled nor looked sorrowful. Her face remained the same.

She said: Oh, Tom was a card. He went away.

Some revellers from the ballroom came in, drunk, singing, wearing paper hats. She said: I must be off.

— I'll see you in the morning.

— I'm off duty then. Because of the late dance tonight. But we hope you'll come back often to see the old places.

— Do you ever remember, he asked, a Fusilier Nixon, a wild fellow.

She thought: No. But there were so many fusiliers. A lot of them we'll never see again.

— We'll look out for you on the teevee, she said.

They shook hands again.

They said goodbye to his mother and drove away. His daughter said: Dad, this isn't the Dublin road.

— There's a place I want to see before we leave.

It was the place that Tom and himself used to go to when they considered that the mental strain of school was too much for them. For it was an odd thing that in all the comings and goings of that railway station nobody ever thought of asking a pair of truants what they were doing there. Everybody thought that everybody else was waiting for somebody else, and there was always porters and postmen who knew what you were at, but who kept the knowledge to themselves, and would share talk and cigarettes with runaway convicts, let alone reluctant schoolboys. No police hunted for drifters or loiterers as in American bus stations: and the sights were superb and you met the best people. They had spent several hours one day with Chief Abidu from southern Nigeria and his Irish wife and honey-coloured brood. He danced on broken glass and swallowed fire in a wooden booth in the Old Market, and, beating on his breast, made the most wonderful throaty noises; and came, most likely, from Liverpool.

— I understand, she had written, that the railway station is closed now. Only the ghosts of those who passed through it abide there. Some were gentle, some were violent men, morose or gay, ordinary or extraordinary. I had time to watch them passing by. It is pain that they died so young, so long ago.

The tracks were gone, the grass and weeds had grown high through the ballast. The old stone buildings had been turned into warehouses. Two men in dusty dungarees kept coming and going, carrying sacks of meal, at the far end of the platform. But if they spoke to each other they were too far away for their voices to be heard, and the cold wind moved as stealthily in grass and weeds as if it were blowing over some forlorn midland hillside. Where the bookstall had been there was just a scar on the granite wall, where she had stood, framed against coloured books and magazines, and watched the soldiers coming and going.

— The young English poet you mention, I knew briefly. He came to buy books. At first he had little to say, simply polite, that's all. Then one day he and another young man began to talk. They included me. But mostly I listened. It was fascinating. After that, when he came he talked about books. He asked questions about Ireland. He was uneasy there, considered it beautiful but alien, felt, I think, that the very earth of Ireland was hostile to him, the landscape had a brooding quality as though it waited.

— He was five or six months garrisoned in our town. They told me he could be very much one of the boys, but he could also be remote. He treated me kindly, teased me gently. But he and a brilliant bitter Welshman gave me books and talked to me. Sometimes they talked about the war.

— It was only after he was reported missing in Africa that I learned he was a poet. But I think I knew anyway.

— I never heard if the Welshman survived. I had several long letters from him and that was all.

Ghosts everywhere in this old town.

— Now I have a son who may pass through a railway station or airport on his way to war.

He said to his daughter: That's where the bookstall was.

— Will you go to see her, dad? In the states, I mean.

— In a way I've seen her.

He was grateful that she didn't ask him what on earth he was talking about.

— As the song says, I'll look for her if I'm ever back that way.

The ghost of his father stood just here, waving farewell to him every time he went back after holidays to college in Dublin.

They walked through the cold deserted hall, where the ticket offices had been, and down the steps, grass-grown, cracked, to the Station Square, once lined with taxis, now empty except for some playing children and the truck into which the dusty men were loading the sacks. From the high steeple the noonday angelus rang.

— How high up is the bell? his son asked.

He told me, and also told him the height of the spire and of the surmounting cross, and why one spire was higher than the other, and how he had once climbed up there, and of the view over the valley, and of how he had almost fallen to doom on the way down, and of the vertigo, the fear of death, that followed.

— And a curious thing. Once, on top of the Eiffel Tower, that vertigo returned. And once over the Mojave desert when I thought the plane was going to crash. But I didn't see Paris or the Mojave desert. I saw that long straight ladder.

The bell ceased. The spires were outlined very clearly in the cold air, looked as formidable as precipices. Around them floated black specks, the unbanishable jackdaws.

— Once I got a job from the parish priest because I was a dab hand with a twenty-two. The job was to shoot the jackdaws, they were pests, off the spires. It was going fine until the police stopped me for using a firearm too close to a public highway. The sexton at the time was a tall man in a black robe down to his feet, more stately than a bishop. One day, when he was watching me at work, a bird I shot struck one of those protruding corner-stones and came soaring, dead, in a wide parabola, straight for the sexton. He backed away, looking in horror at the falling bird. But he tripped on his robe, and the bird, blood, feathers, beak and all got him fair in the face. At the time I thought it was the funniest thing I had ever seen.

— Grisly, his daughter said.

— But once upon a time I laughed easily. It was easy to laugh here then.

High Street, Market Street, the Dublin Road. A stop at the grave where the caretaker's men had already done their job. The weeds were gone, the sad hollow filled, new white stones laid.

Then on to Dublin, crossing the Drumragh at Lissan Bridge where, it was said, Red Hugh O'Donnell had passed on his way back from prison in Dublin Castle to princedom in Donegal and war with Elizabeth of England.

The wintry land brooded waiting, as it had always done, and would do for ever.

He sang at the wheel: There was once a maid in a lovely garden.

— Oh dad, his daughter said.

So he thought the rest of it: Oh, do you see yon high high building? And do you see yon castle fine? And do you see yon ship on the ocean? They'll all be thine if thou wilt be mine.